Respect My Gangsta 4

Bullets Reign

By

Ms. Pantha Jones

TakeOver Publishing LLC

Gary, Indiana

Paperback ISBN#13 978-0-9824338-5-0

Cover Design- LRB

Dedicated to

My Day Ones

Cashmere & Diamond

Your presence has always motivated me to be more and to want more.

My Husband

Antur

Thank you for putting yourself in a position where God can lead you to let be victorious.

Acknowledgements

GOD, GOD, GOD

Thanks to the constant support, Family and Friends.
I will always acknowledge my children and husband
Antur Sr., Tyrin (Shaquan), Diamond, Cashmere, Antur
Jr., Anturnett, Joshua , Angeleah, Kingston. The
Rayford Girls
My Siblings- Loomis and Romancia Arnold.
Dantriece Wilderness

Bland, Little, Arnold, Jones, Brown, Mitchell,
Rimmer, Ammons, Bryant,
        Special Thanks To the Aunts and Uncles. Auntie
Nita, Auntie Re Re, Uncle Billy, Auntie Ann, Auntie
Jean, Auntie Sherry, Uncle Anthony, Uncle Terry,
Auntie Niecey, Uncle French. Auntie Niecey Jones,
Uncle Johnnie, Uncle Marvin, Uncle Larry.
        Special Thanks to The Mitchell Sisters and
family that made my family's transition to a new city
a little easier. I love that my children are
surrounded by family a village of their own. Valerie
Davis, Linda Asim, Montre Moore, Vanessa Little,
Kenyatta Louden, Ladortha Mitchell, Vanessa Mitchell,
Superman, Carlos Mitchell, Cookie, Tony.

I would like to take the time to give a shout out to the Gary, IN's music scene. When I asked for music to write too these are the people who are always right there with it, "What type of music you need?" I tell them what scene I'm working on in a book and BAM, my inbox and email start filling up with links to their music.

Aja Boyd aka Wyld Violetz from book one on TakeOver Pub you always keeps me with it.

Bingo On The Track aka James Cotton, The book of James! Loved it! Kept it on repeat, I didn't have to skip over not one song. Thank you

Billboard Be aka Brandon Bowens of Real Recognize Real Records. Since Book One you were always able to give me something to keep me in killer mode.

Bianca aka B, she is always shouting out other rappers for me to listen to from Gary, In. Love that about her! Keep me current, B!

To the people that I have missed, This Is Not My Last Book!

Respect My Gangsta 4

Bullets Reign

By

Ms. Pantha Jones

Chapter 1

La Petite Mort/ The little death

Sorrow was occupied with her thoughts, thoughts of her son and thoughts of her adulterous husband. She stood there on autopilot as she whisked the eggs and cheese together in a bowl. Malakai eased his way into the kitchen watching her as she stared off into nothingness; silence captured his tongue and captured his body without motion as he was mesmerized by her beauty.

She snapped out of the trance she was in, the hem of his button-down shirt lifted to tease his mind with the cuff of her motherland melanin ass, as she stood on her tippy toes to reach for the pepper. She always loved to wear his button-downs even in the beginning, and he loved her wearing them.

A moan almost escaped his lips at the sight of her; her tousled new short curly hair gave her a sexier mature look. It highlighted her high cheekbones, which was one of his weaknesses. He licked his lips and grabbed his manhood through his gray jogging pants.

Sorrow was unaware of his presence in that present moment because her mind stayed on yesterday and the days before yesterday. She played every scene, every caress, every stroke, every smile and every laugh he gave that bitch and every little bit of it hurt. He was supposed to be different. He had stayed different from the rest since she was 14. What happened to that unbreakable bond they had.

He was supposed to be different.

And she was supposed to be that difference.

She was supposed to be the reason why he wanted himself to be different. Maybe she lost that reason.

 She failed.

 She wonders why do women attack themselves with insecure thoughts? Destroying their image, second-guessing their roles by blaming themselves? Why? He fucked up and cheated. Not her!

He failed.

He failed her.

He failed the marriage.

And she failed to keep him faithful.

Fuck that there she goes again blaming herself.

 Malakai walked over to his wife lifted up the shirt, yanked off her panties and dropped to his knees as if he was worshiping her ass.

In her mind, she wonders why after such a gut-wrenching betrayal do women give up such a precious gift? As, if she is rewarding his acts of unfaithfulness. The pains of her imagination were so profound, the visuals were heartbreaking. The pleasure of his touch tried to distract her pain but it only reminded her that his touches gave someone else pleasure.

Quietly she whispered to herself, "Was it the same pleasure?" She felt the squeeze around her heart tighten, was that pain her intuition telling her, that the same love and feelings her husband had behind giving her pleasure mirrored what he had for Alexus?

Or was it the devil?

"Please, God let it be the devil." The prayer was just a whisper on her lips. But she knew God heard it. God and she could handle the devil trying to control her thoughts. But, if it was her intuition it was the end. Yet still, she wanted to pleasure him in a way that would keep his ass home. To prove to Alexus that this would be the last pussy he would ever have in life. Because, it was the best pussy he ever had in life.

She wonders why would women lodge that in their heads? If that was true, why was he fucking her in the first place? The best pussy doesn't mean shit. In the end, it was just an uneventful attempt to boost their ego. The situation still happened. And you are still left not knowing if he will go back to her again and again. Not even understanding why he went to her in the first place. Sorrow feared those answers. Like most women. But, Sorrow would rather know the truth.

Duke's infidelities were different, it wasn't his unfaithfulness that stirred her emotions it was his disloyalty. She felt anger towards him, she also felt sorry for him. She pitied him, so she stayed. This, this with her husband, his unfaithfulness felt like her spirit was dying. This was a hurt she never felt before. But, she wanted to stay. Why?

He smacked her on the ass jolting her out of her thoughts. That pleasure was painful. It didn't use to be. However, she knew that act was for her to toot her ass out some more. She did and for a minute the sting on her ass was a distraction. His tongue going deeper into her was a chilling goosebumps attack of distraction. It was mere interference from the turmoil that was feasting on her insides.

Did he smack Alexus's ass?

Did she like it more than she did?

Did her ass give him the visual pleasure of jiggling more than hers?

Her wondering was homicidal to her and marriage suicide, it was a game of Russian roulette.

He palmed her ass as his tongue dug deeper.

He told her he loved to see her walk away.

He loved her ass.

She loved that he loved her ass.

He loved her ass in heels and panties.

Is that why he cheated because he loved to see her walk away? She tried to clear her mind because now she was thinking stupid shit.

Please, she pleaded with her mind; push those thoughts into the abyss of forgotten pains.

Forget the pain.

Enjoy him.

Enjoy us as one.

He placed his tongue on her flesh and made soft wet circles on her peach. Sorrow had no choice but to put the bowl of eggs down, as he licked her crack up and down. She arched her back as a shiver ran up and down her spine. He demanded her body to respond with just the tip of his tongue. She smacked her open hands against the cabinet doors. The sting brought her back to reality.

Why is she giving him her body? Again! Succumbing to his attempts to make her forget. She wanted to forget. God knows she wanted to forget.

Euphoric induced amnesia techniques. Was it written somewhere in the cheating mother fuckers' handbook?

Why? She remembers Duke in this moment. Again, she compared the two men. The same tactics to remove betrayal from her mind were used by him. Is it a man thing? Are all men really alike in some way?

Forgetfulness couldn't undo the bond he broke.

He didn't deserve the taste of her yoni on his lips.

How could he?

At a time like this, how could he?

I am in my most vulnerable state.

I needed him to be my strength.

My child is missing.

Our child is missing.

And now my husband is missing.

Where did my family go?

He moved downward towards her Yoni, Malakai tapped her leg, she knew to place it on the countertop, and he placed both his hands on her ass cheeks.

Sorrow grabbed his locks and grinds on his face.

It was a power move. Is this why women engaged in sexual acts with their adulterous husbands and significant others? To gain back their upper hand, to give them a false sense of security, to hide their insecurities? Flashes of him eating Alexus entered her head. She couldn't cum.

But she needed to cum into his mouth; it gave Sorrow solace knowing that his mouth was filled with her. She wanted her cum to erase the taste of any signs of Alexus's he had in his mouth.

His lips were dripping with her.

His taste buds were soaking her up.

His throat was coated with her.

And would she find consolation in knowing that he carried her inside of him, even to her?

The nights and days he thought his secret was safe did he carry Alexus inside of him even to her? Disgust and bile entered her mouth from the pit of her stomach. Would he treat her the same as his side chick? Did everything her brothers taught her about men apply to her husband?

He devoured her until he felt her legs shake and her juices squirt. He was not going to remove his tongue until he savored all of her hurt and removed it from her in the form of her juices.
He made her orgasm.
The little death.
In Shakespearean times that is what they compared an orgasm too. Death! La petite Mort!

"Lanmò a ti kras, ou dwe touye m 'de fwa, renmen mwen?" she whispered upon his ear in her ancestors' native tongue when he came up for a kiss. (The little death, must you kill me twice, my love?)

After the orgasm, she felt empty. She felt as if he had plunged the knife he stabbed her with deeper into her heart. He didn't understand her hurt of his betrayal, the frustration and the longing for her son. He didn't understand the tears that dangled in her eyes. How could there be tears after that, after he had shown her his oral dedication? But how could there not be?

Sex was not a road to forgiveness. It was only a minor fix, an illusion of perfection she no longer believed in. He satisfied his conscience by convincing it that those were tears of joy. She and him being one in the physical form was her showing him forgiveness. It was not.

At this point she felt she had lost everything, her cycle of sorrow has continued no matter what she had done to change herself. No matter how many times she repented, no matter how many times she asked for forgiveness and no matter how many times she had thrown herself on the altar.

Had her past still angered God? Had she not been forgiven? Had she not learned whatever lesson he was trying to teach her? Is she still paying for her father's and mother's sins? Is she still doomed to spend her days living her namesake? So, many questions with no answers. So, many secrets that a husband held from his wife.

Sorrow left Malakai downstairs to finish his second breakfast, with a false sense of satisfaction that he had reconciled with his wife, with just the flick of his tongue. The other night it was the stroke of his dick that made her slumber seemingly peaceful next to him. He had made love to her and tried to explain, without explaining the reasons why she should just trust him on this one. She wonders was this what it was like for Mr. King.

Sorrow breathes a sigh of relief as she closes the bedroom door behind her. She needed to be away from him. She needed to catch her breath. She needed to think, and she couldn't think when she was around him. Clearly, not with visions of the other woman and him corrupting her thoughts. Not with his eyes pleading for understanding of actions he will not justify with answers. He let her follow him, she knew he did. But, why?

Her mind was interrupted by the ringing of a cell phone. She picked it up without thinking, looking at the text message. "Are you still coming over?" Alexus was the name it was under.

She tried to coax herself to just put the phone down before her anger and curiosity got the best of her. Sorrow wasn't this woman. However, she couldn't, she wanted to know what words he had whispered to Alexus via text message when he was with her. What secrets did they form together?

She strolled up, she looked at the time and realized that before he had come downstairs for breakfast, her husband was sexting with Alexus. It was nothing to do with what he will do to her but all about what she will do to him. She didn't care in her mind, this was the reason he was so inclined to give her oral.

The more she thought about it, the more rage took over her rational mindset. "Thiiis mother fucker, she laughed to herself, this mother fucker'" she screamed as she locked the door to the bedroom. She no longer was on the stage of denial, she no longer was on the stage of excuses and self-blame. She was now at the stage of rage.

The rage she thought, why couldn't women end and begin with rage when they have been assaulted with infidelities? Instead, of going through all the other stages of dealing with a cheating spouse.

She went into his walk-in closet, she looked at his clothes, and she started snatching out all of the outfits that he was wearing when he went to that bitch's house. Yes, she remembered them all down to his fucking socks. She paused in the middle of her rampage and decided she needed some fucking theme music for this shit.

This mother fucker must have forgotten who the fuck she was, no she had forgotten who she was, "Echo play Don't hurt yourself by Beyoncé, in every room."

Malakai

Downstairs eating his breakfast and reading the paper with a smile on his face. He heard the start of a song coming through the speakers in the kitchen. That was usual of his wife, she loved music. The volume had risen as Beyoncé belted out, *Who the fuck do you think I is? You ain't married to no average bitch, boy, You can watch my fat ass twist, boy, As I bounce to the next dick, boy."*

"What the fuck?" he dropped his fork. This wasn't her just listening to music, this was his wife sending his ass a message. A message that he thought he avoided. Malakai started searching for his wife, it would be a difficult task because every room was playing the same fucking song. He decided to start in the basement and work his way up to the top of the house.

Sorrow

Upstairs Sorrow was being empowered by the edgy hard rock sound of Beyoncé belting out her truth, "*And keep your money, I got my own, Keep a bigger smile on my face being alone,*"

Sorrow stuffed the shit he had worn to be with Alexus in their big circle Jacuzzi tub, "*Bad motherfucker, God complex. Motivate your ass, call me Malcolm X,*" she poured a whole bottle of bleach on top of his garments and shoes. "*Yo operator, or innovator*

Fuck you, hater, you can't recreate her, no You'll never recreate her no, hell no." Sliding on a pair of torn booty shorts under Malakai's button down shirt. She hurriedly slipped on her thigh high leather boots. "*We just got to let it be, Let it be, let it be, let it be, baby,*" she then ran to grab her roll away suitcase, "*You just got to let it be. Let it be, let it be, let it be, babe.*" Running around the room she quickly threw her belongings into the suitcase. "*When you*

hurt me, you hurt yourself. Don't hurt yourself.
When you diss me, you diss yourself
Don't hurt yourself. When you love me, you love
yourself. Love God herself."

She then set her suitcase by the locked bedroom door. She runs to the bathroom singing the lyrics, "*I am the dragon breathing fire,*" she throws the match into the tub, igniting his tainted clothes.

"*Beautiful mane, I'm the lion,*" She puts her hair under running water from the faucet, running her fingers to style it, she now hears faint knocking on the bedroom door. "*Beautiful man, I know you're lying, I am not broken, I'm not crying, I'm not crying.*"

Sorrow hears the fire; she smells the burning of adultery assaulting her sense of smell. She grabs her makeup and applies black lipstick to her lips. She continues to sing as she slays her look and laugh at the now angry beats at the door.

"Ha, you mad! Who gives a fuck about your fucking feelings? Not I says the cat. "She says as she blows herself a kiss. She was outside herself or was she? She was in love with Malakai had been since she was 14, never fall in love with anyone but him. Her brothers had taught her how to treat every unfaithful man but never one that she was in love with. Never one that she exchanged vows with in front of God. No, they never taught her that.

"*You ain't trying hard enough You ain't loving hard enough You don't love me deep enough We not reaching peaks enough Blindly in love, I fucks with you 'Til I realize I'm just too much for you, I'm just too much for you.*"

She grabs Malakai's blunt off the nightstand, she sees a paper that says he is 100% the father of a child. She lights the blunt in the doorway of the bathroom and laughs. Was this really her fucking life? She was convulsed with laughter. Her son was gone and this nigga goes and replaces him with another bitch's baby. "Ah, why the fuck not?" she said out loud. Sorrow chortles harder as if she was delirious. Crying was no longer an action she would entertain.

Sorrow was surrounded by rage, she was facing the rage of the burning fire, at her back was the rage of angry kicks and punches at the door but that didn't even compare to the vexation that was inside of her. The lyrics and hard rock beat of Beyoncé was the raging theme music to it all. She was insanely delighted. She didn't feel like herself. Or was this herself just in another form.

Why didn't every woman who had been wronged, cheated on, betrayed feel like this song? She felt as if this song should be the only stage, fuck all the other stages. She puts the blunt out, and she continues to sing along, *"We just got to let it be Let it be, let it be, let it be, let it be, babe."*

She grabs her suitcase, she swings the door open and she is face to face with her husband, while still singing, *"Uh, this is your final warning, You know I give you life,"* she pulls off her ring and drops it on the ground and smashes into the floor with the boots she only wears when she is fucking him. *"If you try this shit again, You gon' lose your wife."*

Malakai

Malakai was pissed but when she opened that door the look on her face told him, don't try me.

Her attire and her new edgy look let him know that she was walking out a different woman. This is what your betrayal caused this is what my hurt looks like, mother fucker. It was undeniable showing from every cell in her body.

Sorrow advertised it; she was screaming it in his face without really saying a word. The song said it all, what she had on said it all and the look on her face dared you to say it didn't. The fire coming out of the opening of their tub showed him this is what her hurt was capable of doing.

Hell yeah, he wanted to curse her ass out. Tell her to pick up her damn ring and change her clothes. He would be damned if she walked out of this looking as if she had nothing on, with the boots he bought that was only reserved for his pleasure. Those were her Fuck'em Girl boots.

But, how could he ,knowing that he was hurting her but refuse to tell her why?

He knew that his actions caused this chaos. He couldn't tell her baby it's not what you think when clearly he has fucked Alexus. How would it sound if he said baby I'm fucking her for all the right reasons? It sounded like bullshit.

However, she was going to hear what he had to say. Even if it wasn't the truth she wanted to hear. He looked at the fire once again; it still was maintained inside of the tub. Right then Malakai knew nothing but the whole truth would make her stay. But, he couldn't. He couldn't tell her because he knew she would go right into kill mode and she couldn't do that just yet. So, instead, he grabbed her waist with one arm to stop her from passing him, "Look at me. "

Sorrow reluctantly looked up at her husband, the love of her life, her first love, her best friend and now the cause of this pain on top of pain. Malakai saw the flicker of hurt in her eyes that was masked by rage. She saw the pain in his eyes, guilt with regret. But right now she could give two fucks about how he felt. She stopped and listened anyway, hoping he would tell her at least why.

"Nobody in this mother fucking world is vital enough for me to betray your trust except for OUR SON! This shit right here is for forever. He said picking up her ring and placing it in her hand, Til death do us part. So, I understand that you need your space right now. You have every right to be mad. But, know once this shit is all over, you lay your head wherever I lay my head." Malakai let her go.

"Actions speak louder than words. And your actions my dear husband is not sitting well with me. Besides, you have your son to focus on and I have my son to focus on." She said smashing the DNA test against his chest and walked away just like that. Sorrow would not let her tears cascade down her cheeks, and she couldn't bring herself to turn around with her head in La La land and deny what she had seen for weeks with her own eyes.

As she put her suitcase in the trunk, she received a text message, "New Instructions-*Drop the money off at your place of business still. But, I want a 100,000 each placed in four black gym bags, and the rest of the money stuffed in a black garbage bag. Place the four gym bags into another black garbage bag. Place both trash bags in the back of your store. And I only want Sorrow to do it.*"

Sorrow got behind the wheel and she exhaled to calm her rage, she wanted to kill everybody at this point. She thought about Hunter and Semaj and her rage sizzled down to anger and it fueled her to think logically. She was not in the right position to curse this asshole out. And she hated that but all in due time.

As she drove Sorrow thought those days of keeping secrets were over. Her heart was surrounded by agony and those walls were sealed shut with anger. She knew if she would have stayed, she would lose her sanity. Being insane with jealousy and hate were not feelings she was use too. She was not prepared for this at a time where they should have been solid as a rock. She couldn't let his infidelity eat away at her mind. She would lose herself.

She would lose her focus.

She would become powerless.

And she could not do that to her son.

She could not do that to her niece. And she refused to do that to herself.

Regardless of what reasons MG had behind his actions with Alexus. A bond had been broken and she didn't know if they could ever get that back. He was keeping something from her that she knew had to be important that was surrounded by Alexus. So, she had to ask herself was it that he was being unfaithful or was it that she thought he was being disloyal, that made her act out the way she did?

Sorrow keeps questioning herself, on why did she fuck him after catching him cheating? And then turned around and shared a part of herself with him again. Was it some type of strategy that we women have, by doing this shit? She couldn't see the reason why, when she knew that visions of them together would invade her mind every time she touched or looked at him.

No, wife wanted to feel that pain nor see the infidelity of the man who was supposed to lead her. Unfortunately, she had to watch him fuck another woman over and over again in her head. And the bitch was the help.

Now, she knew Alexus had a motive for coming to work for her. She had a feeling her motive was more than getting to Malakai. She wanted to kill her, she had a change to kill her but she didn't. Then they supposedly had a child together. How old was this child? How was she supposed to forgive him? Fuck him and fuck that. Maybe she should make them even. An eye for an eye, a fuck for a fuck, she would repent later.

Pushing Malakai to the back of her mind, she drove to Walmart to purchase the items she needed.

Before Sorrow emptied the money out of the safe, she took a picture of her Grandme's watermark, she sent the picture to everyone even Genesis. They knew if anyone used this money in large sums they were involved in the kidnapping or came in contact with the people who were. They were to be questioned and killed.

Sorrow didn't even try any clever scheme to trap whoever was going to pick the money up. She was going to play nice, abide by the rules and place everything just like the asshole asked. She wanted her son and niece back so once again she would have to swallow her pride and her kill mode to ensure their safe return home.

After the drop she headed to Illinois, she wanted to feel closer to her son. She wanted to dwell in the place where she took care of her son every day. It was where and when her family was complete.

Chapter 2

Climbing out of the Uber, it's a good thing somebody left her cell phone along with other items in the closet in the hospital room. Her mind was doing a checklist of what she was going to need. Genesis slowly lifted her legs one at a time up the stairs to her apartment. Entering her apartment, flashes hit her, the bottom of a Timberland coming down on her head.

She winced.

The punches and stomps glued her to that day.

She moved around her apartment slowly looking for the morphine pills she had hidden from Sabrina after having surgery on her knee about 6 months ago when she was in that car accident. She still had a full bottle somewhere.

She tried hard to remember where it was, the secret compartment in the medicine cabinet. She eased her way towards the bathroom, holding on to the walls. She stopped to catch her breath and to let the pain subside a little.

She noticed once she entered there were things missing. She looked around; Sabrina's personal items were missing. Why?

Her expensive ass shampoo and conditioner.
Gone.
Her expensive ass bathrobe hanging behind the door.
Gone.
Where was Sabrina when everything went down?
Gone.

Where was Sabrina now?

Gone.

Genesis ran some bath water, took out an outfit. She slowly took her jogging suit off, no panties or bra to worry about; she didn't have time to put those on before she left.

Fully naked she sees the almost faded bruises and lumps she had decorating her body like tattoos. She felt the Morphine ease the pain in her body. She lowered her body into the soothing hot water.

Closing her eyes, she dunks her head all the way in, covering the crown of her head. Flashes of that day attack her mind once again. This would be a memory she would never forget. This will be something her mind and body would feel forever.

Her eyes popped open to the realization that Sabrina knew.

Sabrina never takes her son just to run to the store. She wouldn't have stopped him from having breakfast. If she could get away with leaving her son with someone, she would. Sabrina almost never took her son if Genesis was at home. Cameron had on the same clothes from that night before.

Why would she let him sleep in his clothes? He lived with them, therefore, he had a gang of pajamas in his room. Besides, Cameron almost threw fits when he couldn't put on his PJ 's. How could she have not seen her odd behavior?

How did they get in the house?

The door was unlocked.

There was no knock.

There was no hard bam of something busting down her door.

Why was her door unlocked? How did they get inside of the building?

Sabrina.

Where was Sabrina?

Gone.

This bitch has to die.

She didn't need to be just gone, she didn't to make her disappear.

She had to call Sorrow.

Damn, the kids.

She tried to hop out of the tub to grab her phone off the side of the sink, she realized that her body still was not ready for that. She had to catch her balance. She put it on speaker as she listened to the messages.

She hears Sorrow, frantic messages.

The kids were still missing.

They were Kidnapped.

Ransom.

Sabrina.

That bitch has to die.

Genesis left in her car to stay at club Black Reign, somewhere people wouldn't look. She knew they were still at a standstill because she was the one that needed to get the Liquor license for the club. It was somewhere safe and secluded. She parked her car at a hotel behind the club and walked with a roll around suitcase full of comfort items.

A suitcase full of guns, ammo, and weed was all she needed. All the other essentials were already in her office at the club.

She had to recuperate herself before killing. She felt too guilty to get in touch with her friends. She wanted to right her fuck up. She should have heeded the hood's warning of Sabrina. She needed to right the wrong of bringing a treacherous, jealous, greedy, trifling ass whore into her family. She wasn't going to stop until she could show up with her head in her hands and the whereabouts of the children. She was not going to contact them until she knew who and where those responsible were located.

Sorrow

"They said when the morning nurse came in to do her vitals, she was gone." Sorrow whispered into the phone.

"I'm going to go to her house and the apartment in Small Farms," Nigel said.

Sorrow hung up the phone and went back to the nurse's station where Genesis's parents were talking to the Hospital staff. They were going to put out a missing person's report. Genesis's health was unstable, they were still unsure of her internal damage. Let alone her state of mind.

Watching and listening Sorrow's mind wondered. Did Genesis have something to do with the kidnapping? Why disappear? Why didn't she contact them? She had a lot of questions but only Genesis had the answers.

Genesis was the key to everything.

Sorrow called Truth.

No answer.

This bitch stays MIA, Sorrow ended her unanswered call shaking her head.

She looked at the time, it was time for her to go meet that nigga from Dorie Miller.

Chapter 3

The horrifying dream scared Truth awake, she jumped out of the bed. She started punching her fist into her open hand, pacing the floor.

Darkness. Loneliness.

Even though Sorrow took her on a ride along to Alexus house, she knew it was tension still between them. She had said some hurtful things to her best friend. Things that she hasn't really apologized to her for saying. That's why she was keeping her distance from the Miller house. Weed and liquor took her to a place where didn't want to go, that is why she never smoked weed when she got older. It turned her into something.

Pure Darkness blanketed the silence in her room.

No laughter.

No soft voice of a little girl just learning to use full sentences.

No lavender and vanilla smell of her baby girl filling the house.

No vision of her baby girls beautiful honey-colored face.

No Baby Girl.

Has she changed in the last month?

All they heard was the distant crying sounds of their children.

The cries of the children calling out for them, made her heart sank more and more into a black hole. "Mommy! Daddy! Come get me!

Tears stumbled out

Tears of regret.

She loved her daughter.

But for some reason, she was scared to be a mother.

She was scared of fucking up her daughter.
Like her mother fucked her up or how Chenille fucked up Sorrow.

She paced back and forth in her bedroom. She stopped and looked around realizing that her husband was once again not at home or just not sleeping in their bed with her. More than likely he was at the Miller house or out of town setting up that Underground Playgrounds shit.
No soft snores.

The warmth and security of his body had disappeared from her side. Too many times since the kidnapping he hasn't been home and when he did come home he slept in their daughter's room.

She would sleep beside him tonight, even if that meant lying beside him in their daughter's twin size Princess and the Frog canopy bed.

Truth laughed as she walked to her daughter's bedroom. Semaj loves Princess and The Frog movie. A smile grew as she thought of her child watching that movie over and over again.

It used to irritate her.

Now, Truth longed for it.

She wanted to hear her daughter's 2-year-old soft voice sing along.

She needed it. She checked in her daughter's bedroom.

No Nigel.

Disappointment set in, as she lit her blunt and popped two Xanax, washing it down with a glass of wine.

She never used to pop pills. She refused to take it for her postpartum depression. She wanted to fight that shit on her own and she did with weed and drinking.

But, that nightmare terrified her common sense. It invaded her mind until she couldn't concentrate on anything else. She needed something to make that nightmare release her mind from its hold. Weed or drinking alone could not stop the visuals in her head, Xanax would do the trick. Xanax would be her savior.

Truth shook her head. But for some reason, the vision of Teesha taking her daughter in that nightmare stuck with her.
Questions popped into her head.
Why did she want Nigel Jr. to go to Haiti's with them, so bad? Knowing they weren't taking any of the children.
Why didn't the kidnappers take Nigel Jr.?

Not that she wanted them to take him. But, that was a valid question that turned over in her head.
Why did Teesha get so nice all of a sudden?

Wanting to talk to her like she had some sense, instead of the sarcastic ass, "My Baby Daddy. Please," Whenever she called the house phone or Truth's phone. No greeting with her bitter ghetto ass. Truth rolled her eyes at the thought.

In fact, she felt like the bitch was asking too many questions, now. She felt like she was too concerned for her child. Jr. use to come back from home and ask his dad," Why doesn't mommy like for me to tell her about the fun I have with my sister." Hmph, cause that hoe mad! She wanted to say but bit her tongue because of the love she had for Nigel Jr.

She wasn't asking Nigel any questions about the situation but she was asking her. That in itself was odd behavior for Teesha. She jumped at every chance she got to converse with Nigel. Now,

52

all of a sudden she wanted to call her and play nice. Bullshit!

Why, though?

When Teesha's goal in life is to get Nigel back or make their life difficult since she can't. Why was she treating her like her best friend? Why was she distancing herself from him, now?

What is this conniving hiding?

And why is she so adamant about Jr. staying with her mother down south all of a sudden. When was she just so gung-ho about him being with us? Why isn't she down there with her son?

Visions of Teesha standing over her daughter with a sinister grin started flashing in her head.

"Mommmmmmmmy, an angelic voice called out to her sound as if it was coming from outside of the house. In her sleeping shorts, tank top, and flip-flops; hair in a bonnet Truth was reading to get to the bottom of things. She laughed at herself, if anyone who knew Truth saw her, they would have known something was not right. She never goes anywhere without her hair done, let alone walk outside in a bonnet or scarf on her head.

She was hallucinating her daughter's voice all the way to Teesha's house. The closer and closer she drove to her house, the louder her daughter's voice had gotten.

Her daughter seemed to be calling her through the walls of Teesha's house. Truth took her butcher's knife out of the glove compartment. Wait. Now, that Truth was thinking about it, *who in the hell told her about the kids? They were keeping the shit on the hush hush. Since Nigel Jr. was down south Nigel did not have a reason to tell Teesha anything.*

She texted, Nigel-"Did you tell Teesha about the kids?"
"Hell Naw!" he texted back.

"When did Teesha's mom say Teesha drove him down there?" she texted.

"Her mom called me while we were in Haiti. Said that she was making sure everything was okay because Teesha was acting as if something was going on. I told her, it probably was because he was on school break and he was supposed to stay with us, but we were out of the country."

"Why are you asking all these questions about that crazy ass female?" texted again

Truth ignored his question and started texting again.

She texted, "Thank you, Teesha for checking on me all the time. Mother to mother I appreciate it. It's a good thing Nigel told you about it. I guess that's why you decided to send Jr. down south? Great thinking, we wouldn't anything to happen to him also."

Truth glanced up at Teesha's house, that bitch was still up; she saw her prancing around with something in her hand and her phone. She could see right through the stupid bitch's curtains. This bitch was counting money, a stack of money!

Teesha texted back, "Yeah, I'm glad when Nigel came back he told me. I drove him down there a couple of days after you guys came home. I was scared shitless of someone taking him also. I can just imagine what you are going through."

Truth can see Teesha still dancing and prancing around. Truth stepped out the car to get a better visual. Truth grabbed Nigel's set of keys to Teesha's house that she gave him for emergencies. "Yeah, right, Truth thought, Teesha was hoping his ass used it for other late night reasons.

Truth despised Teesha's type; she didn't have any respect for Marriage. Luckily, her husband does honor their vows and he never fell for the bullshit Teesha was trying to throw his way.

Truth needed to find out what this bitch knew. Watching Teesha leave the living room, Truth crept into the back of her house to find it dark. She stuck the key in and gently opened the door. She was careful not to make any noise, she bent down beside the kitchen and she listened to the sounds of the house.

Teesha sounded like she was in the upstairs bathroom. Truth tiptoed to the living room, lying on the table was a stack of large bills and a black gym bag. Truth heard a nose above her head.

She didn't wait to see if she had enough time to look at money, she quickly eased her way back out of the house and went back to her car. She grabbed a bottle of wine out of her trunk. She stepped back to the front door with the butcher's knife in her purse, just in case; she put a fake smile on her face and rung the bell.

Nigel had expressed disgust at Teesha's attitude and behavior when she was intoxicated. She had gotten him into plenty of fights with her mouth when they used to be together. Somehow the bitch grew a cape, muscles and developed diarrhea at the mouth when she would drink.

Truth plan was to keep her cool until she let something slip out about the kids or when she saw the money. She was going to text the others to come to Teesha's house and they all would take it from there.

Teesha was puzzled as to who would be at her door this hour, she ran downstairs to the living room and hurriedly threw the money back into the bag. She then threw the bag behind the couch. Truth was peeking through the side window and saw where she threw the bag. Truth reached into her purse and gripped the handle of her knife. Just in case, she coaxed herself, only just in case.

Answering the door Teesha was taken aback by Truth, Truth took note that Teesha was beet red and had a scared look on her face when she was at her the door.

"What'chu doing here?" she questioned as she looked outside to see if anybody else was present. Her heartbeat was racing, her palms started sweating.

Truth held up her bottle of wine, "Came for a little girl talk."

Teesha didn't know what else to do so, ushered her in, "I'll pop the top and get the glasses." she stated as she took the wine from her. "Deep breaths, Deep breaths, she said to herself in the kitchen as she put her back against the wall. If I ask this bitch to leave she might get suspicious, Teesha was the one that kept texting her and told her anytime she wanted to talk her door was open.

Truth only smiled and sat down. She looked around the room, burnt oranges, browns and hints of green decorated her home. It had given her a warm feeling but she dares not let her guard down with this one, Teesha had her fire roaring in the fireplace. Truth actually liked her taste. It's a damn shame her and Teesha could never be friends not even for the sake of their children. Old bitter bitch!

"You know what's funny, Teesha beamed as she walked back into the room, I never would have thought you would come outside all regular and shit. "

"Mmmm, she put the glass to her lips, regular? I don't think so; even at my worst I would never be regular." She corrected her with a chuckle.

Teesha ignored her uppity remark, "So, are you closer to finding Semaj and Hunter?" She held her breath in anticipation.

"No."

"Damn, that's fucked up. I know dealing with Nigel you guys haven't involved the police. Have you?" Teesha said digging.

Truth just nodded her head.

"That's what I lovvve about Nigel, Teesha said with a longing in her voice, he always handles his business. Teesha fanned herself as a memory of her & Nigel fucking came into play.

Teesha must not have realized that Truth was not drinking. Teesha had let the alcohol pump her chest up enough that her true feelings about Nigel and she had come out. Truth knew it wouldn't take long she already saw her drinking while she was texting her.

"The funniest shit is, this nigga never fell for my seduction. I have tried everything; all the things I knew turned him on. I know we in

62

competition but bitch do you see this, she said standing up and turning around. "Come on I'm the fucking shit. But, Nothing. Nada. But, that nigga used to always fuck other bitches when we were together. But he never would cheat on you." she giggled almost done with the whole bottle.

"Is that so?" Truth said nonchalantly raising one eyebrow as she gripped her butcher knife. She had to release it, because the more this bitch talked, the more she wanted to slit her throat.

"Hell yeah, I thought I had a chance even tho, Y'all got married. Girl, I am not about fucking a married man. Sorry, Not sorry. You feel me? Shit, besides who the fuck is going to trump the woman who has his seed, Right! I know my pussy is good shit, he made sure he nutted all up in it, to have Nigel Jr." She was giggling and talking about Nigel as if Truth was not his wife. Yet, still, Truth kept calm and nursed her glass of wine.

Teesha continued, "Even with you guys getting married, I knew I would have chances to break your shit up. He had to deal with me, rather he liked it or not. I felt like the girl off Baby Boy, that Tyrese wouldn't fuck. You know the one she said standing up, imitating the actress, "You know you want this pussy!" SHIIIIIIT!" Teesha starts pacing the floor getting animated and more reckless. Truth's anger caused her to shake her leg.

Keeping her hate caged was becoming more and more difficult as she listened to her talk. Truth was still hearing her daughter's angelic voice crying out to her from Teesha's womb.

"Then you had to become pregnant and have the very thing he wanted and I wanted after we had Nigel. A girl. A mother fucking girl and named her one of the names he said he wanted to name our baby girl. Semaj. Semaj. Semaj." She chants with hatred dripping from her daughter's name, That nigga always wanted a girl." she laughed stumbling, her words now showing her hatred.

Again Truth stayed focused on what she needed from her before she stabbed the bitch a hundred times for saying her daughter's name like that.

"I thought God had said fuck me. Shit, this bitch got his name, his child, and her own fucking money. She doesn't need his shit like you do. But then, she smiles with her face lifted up towards the sky, and did a fake dance as if she had the Holy Ghost, this shit happens," she said laughing. Teesha went behind her couch pulling out money and throwing it at Truth.

"What shit happened, Truth said as she grabbed one of the bills and compared it to the picture Sorrow sent to her. It matched. Truths rising out of her chair letting the knife fall into her purse. She asked again through clenched teeth, "What shit happened?"

Teesha looked at Truth sternly trying to keep her eyes focused on her, "Bitch, I kidnapped your daughter. And I'm so glad he didn't want my child, he wanted your-"

Truth leaped on Teesha yanking her head down into her glass coffee table. Glass shattered everywhere cutting Truth and Teesha. Disoriented for a few seconds, with blood dripping from her head. Teesha instantly grabbed the wine bottle sending it flying against Truth's head.

Staggering Truth tries for her purse. Teesha grabs her by her ankle tripping her causing her to fall face first into the glass. Truth felt the sting of the bits of glass cut into her face.

Truth starts kicking Teesha. She cursed herself for wearing flip -flops.

Her kicks were weak allowing Teesha to get a firmer grip to pull her towards her. Truth flips herself over peddling with constant kicks to Teesha's face.

Leaving her with no choice but to let go of her ankle and protect her face. Truth scooted herself backward through jagged pieces of glass. Reaching her purse as Teesha jumped on top of her, losing her balance Teesha fell flat. Before she could raise her body up the knife was plunged into her back.

That didn't stop her, and it didn't stop Truth from constantly plunging the knife into her back. Teesha felt what seemed like hard punches leaving a searing pain. Blood was pouring out of her back, as she falls to the side of Truth.

Truth straddled her holding the knife with both hands she repeatedly thrust the blade into her torso, "Where is my baby?" she screamed before each stabbing. Truth didn't care that blood was gushing out of gaping holes. All she heard was her baby crying to her from Teesha's womb. Sweat and blood dripped from her forehead.

Convinced that there was no sign of life Truth collapsed on the floor out of exhaustion. Her adrenaline was no longer her friend, that blow to the head finally hit her as she passed out in the presence of blood, broken glass and her husband's dead baby momma.

Damn, she fucked up!

Chapter 4

"This stupid bitch!" he cursed as he rushed to Teesha's house. Listening to her confessions, hearing the deadly struggle sent him into a rage. If the bitch wasn't dead, he was going to kill her himself. He couldn't kill Truth. He didn't want anyone from Sorrow's team to get off easy. And death was too easy. The slow torture of watching them fall apart because of their missing children was the pain that his Beloved wanted. And that was what she was going to get.

Branson entered the house through the back, with a gun in hand he maneuvered to the living room. This would be one gruesome crime scene had he still been on the force. Open and shut case. He holstered his gun. He didn't even bother to see if Teesha was still alive. His professional eye he counted over 20 stab wounds.

"Dumb black bitch," he said as he stepped over her body. He checked Truth's pulse.

Still alive.

Good!

He hurriedly went into the dining room and grabbed a rug. He rolled Teesha's body into it, carrying it to his truck. He went back in to collect the bag and the money that was scattered in the bloody mess. He ran through the house opening each drawer, turning over mattresses, searching through cabinets and closets.

No more money to be found.

Good!

He was making sure none of it would lead back to him. He called Bobbie, "Where is your cousin?"

"Where is my money?"

"I'm not giving you shit until you find your cousin."

"That's some fucking bullshit; I held my end of the bargain. I want my money," she screamed into the phone

"Hell, no! Your money will be held until Sabrina shows up. That way I know that my cover was not blown and your cousin didn't snitch. Now, Like I told you before little black man bitch. You will get your money when you show up with her."

He ended the call.

He wasn't about to let anything else go wrong. He bugged everybody's house that was involved, with the exception of Sabrina and Alexus. He didn't get a chance to bug Sabrina because she didn't have a place to stay so when she disappeared, she was able to get off his radar.

Alexus wasn't bugged because his Beloved said that Alexus would do anything that she told her too. She wasn't concerned with her day to day activities. To Thomas, she seemed gullible, love stricken and too trusting.

Truth

Truth jolts up, her memory was a little foggy. She tried to gather herself as the taste of old blood invaded her taste buds. She immediately touched her throbbing head as she tries to stand. She looks around at the scattered broken glass and the puddles of blood on the floor. She remembers. She looks around for Teesha's dead body.

She was gone.

Her body was gone.

Panic overcame her as she frantically looked for her phone in her purse.

Who should she call?

Sorrow?

Nigel?

What would Nigel say? What would he think of her? That she was a pill-popping drunk lunatic. No. She told herself shaking the doubt out of her head.

She had a logical reason as to why she killed her. Or did she just let her emotions get the best of her? What if the stupid bitch was just trying to get under her skin? If she was she pick the wrong subject to fuck her with, she was not playing with anybody about her child.

But, she still didn't get the answers she needed.

Where were the children?

Who had her daughter?

Teesha knew she was sure of it!

She said, "He", in her drunken rant.

And she had the money with the watermark on it.

She had to be involved. Her homicide was justified.

She looked around for the bag.

Gone.

She looked around for the loose money Teesha threw at her.

Gone.

Her weapon.

Gone.

Damn, she fucked up. Tears gathered in her eyes, her heart was racing, the fear of jail seeped into her mind. But, that fear was minor compared to not knowing where her child was. Not knowing if she was safe! Or worse.

Dead.

What will they think of her, without a body and no proof?

She had to call somebody.

Sorrow?

Nigel?

Fuck it, she said as she dialed a number on her cell while grabbing her things and heading out the door. They picked up.

"I killed Teesha. She's dead." She cried frantically into the phone.

"Why? What the fuck happened?"

"I came over here just to talk to her. Teesha lied about when she sent Jr. down south. I wanted to know why she lied, so I came over here to get some answers. She was drinking and she told me out of her mouth that she had Semaj kidnapped. Then she threw money at me and it had the mark. I know that was the ransom money in the black bag. I swear it had the mark. So, we started fighting, she sobbed and I stabbed her." There was a pause, "Where are you now?"

"Going to my car."

"Stay in the car. Don't go anywhere."

 "Ok, she said in shock as she looked down at her blood covered body."

"Don't worry I'm going to clean up the mess. Where is her body located?"

Truth sobbed louder, "I don't know, she stuttered, where the body is located?"

"Wait, I thought you said you killed her?"

"I did."

"How do you know she is dead if there isn't a body? "

"Because, I stabbed her 26 1/2 times, front and back. Ain't no coming back from that. I might not be an expert killer but I know ain't nobody coming back from that."

"Then how the fuck you don't know where the body is located?

"I must have passed out from the blow to my head. When I awoke she was gone and the money with the mark."

"Unfuckingbelievable." the person paused. "Just stay in your car. I will be there."
"Okay"

Truth ended the call. But panic still pulled at her mind. Taunting it with questions. Would they believe her? Would she get caught? Would she go to jail? No, No she reasoned with her head. Tears filled her eyes, "Can't believe I killed that stupid bitch.

Meanwhile at the Underground Playgrounds

"Man, it's some riff-raff in here tonight," China whispered to Ghost as she eyed the men that she was dancing for.
Ghost laughed, "How you know?"

"I sniff out new money, old money, fake money, a nigga that ain't ever had any money and the nigga's getting money. So, trust me, girl, I know." she laughed, and held out one of the bills.

Ghost grabbed the bill.

"See, What money you know got a watermark like this?" she said pointing to the symbol.

Ghost pulled out her cell to look at the picture Sorrow sent to her. It was a match. Ghost tried calling Sorrow.

No answer. Ghost started recording them and sent the video to Nigel and Malakai.

"See, fake money and they have the nerves to be disrespectful," China said in disgust.

As Ghost waited for instructions she gave a money marker to China after she marked the money. China looked at it with a smile, "Ah a get money bitch can be wrong sometimes." she said as she strutted her ass back over to where they were.

Jah walked up to Ghost and watched the men also. Ghost watched as Roc Vega walked over there with a smile.

"Chocolate Cocaine, you are needed elsewhere, baby"

None of the girls challenged Vega; they just did what he said. China didn't like that she had to leave the men now that she knew their money was good. She knew not to cross a Boss.

"See you later fellas. She winked at them as she gathered up the money they were throwing at her.

"Damn that bitch was fine," Kameron said. He was disappointed she left.

"No doubt, no doubt, Big Dawg, Vega said. However, we accommodate the big spenders in a different area. And we here at the Underground Playgrounds like to give our big spenders an Elite type of experience. He pulled out a special bottle of Don Julio Anejo 1942, and said, You feel me!"

"Yeah, Yeah, Kameron started feeling himself, Elite experience. I like that. "All four men poured themselves a drink basically guzzling their glasses of it down until the bottle was gone.

Roc Vega shook his head as he watched them. These niggas have no class, Vega thought to himself.

"Now, that you have had the elite spirit experience. Let's get to that elite pussy experience. Follow me, gentlemen!" Vega led them into a separate room in the warehouse. He opened the door for them to lead them deeper and deeper away from the other clientele.

The four men in their arrogance never questioned the darkness and the lack of other elite clientele, or why Vega was no longer leading them but he was following them with a disgusted look on his face. The feeling of the special Don Julio started to take effect.

Vega had known MG and The King brothers from back in the day when he started off working for C-note. He had nothing but love for them, so to know that these fuck boys might be associated with the kidnapping of their children sent him into a rage. He was all too happy to give them a bottle laced with Hemlock.

Entering into a dark room, with a spotlight on four chairs the men gladly sat down, the alcohol was taking its effect. They weren't so sure what was happening to their bodies or if their drunken state of mind was playing tricks on them.

Their bodies became stiff, paralyzed but they were aware of everything around them. Fear of the unknown was kicking in, questioning their tolerance for elite alcohol. They could not turn their heads but they could move their eyes, they could speak. But, an escape or attack on Vega was not possible.

"What the fuck did you do to us?" Kameron questioned.

Vega laughed as he opened the back door to the warehouse.

When the four men saw who entered, one pissed himself, while the others were paralyzed with fear.

Nigel, Malakai, Vega, and Jah walked over to where the men were sitting. Nigel pulled out a 9mm, Malakai pulled out a black bag, while Vega and Jah stood in the back of the four men with their guns aimed at their heads. Ready to take fire if the Hemlock wore off too soon, one dome shot will be their fate.

"You already know why we are here. The look on your faces tells it all. The look of horrifying terror is adamant. You don't know us. Maybe you heard of us back in the day. But, you don't have any reason to fear us, unless you know what we came here for." MG told the four men.

"Where the fuck is our children? And you, he pointed to Kameron, I have seen you before. And once I figure it out I'm going to make sure I torture and kill everybody you love." Nigel promised.

Malakai pulled out a machine gun out of the black bag and had it aimed at one of the four men, Nigel had his aimed at Kameron. Vega and Jah came around the front of the men and followed suit aiming at the other two.

"Now, you can tell me how did you come about this money or you can see how many bullets it takes to kill you. It's up to you."

"We are going to ask you the question again. Where are our children?" Nigel questioned.

"Where did you get the money from?" MG asked

Kameron had one decision to make, did he fear jail or death? He knew he shouldn't have fucked with Sabrina's dirty ass. His baby momma kept him in some bullshit. The other three men looked on to Kameron to see if he would talk.

Teesha's two cousins were just hanging with the other two because they wanted to get into the Underground Playgrounds. Teesha's cousins weren't about to snitch, Nigel never met them so he had no indication of who they were.

There was dead silence.

Nigel, Malakai, Vega, and Jah all stepped forward in unison and aimed at their particular target.

Guns are drawn. Instead of using the machine gun, MG pulled out his 45.

BANG. Bang. Bang. Bang.

All four men screamed in agony as the gunshots entered the flesh of their feet.

They wanted to look down but the hemlock was still hindering their movements. "Look all we know is some redhead was supposed to leave the door open to her girlfriend's apartment beat her ass, and then wait to get paid. We didn't take your children." a confession made in anguish and pain tends to ring in truth.

"See now we are getting somewhere. That means you are Kameron! Nigel said walking towards him, that's where I know your ass from that bitch, Sabrina."

Waving his gun at Kameron, "You and that bitch are too simple to orchestrate this type of shit. So, who approached you with the kidnapping?"

Through pain, Kameron spoke, "She said this old white cop came to her about it. I don't know shit else."

"So, no one knows where our children are, right? Malakai spoke.

The four men, said No!

"Ok, Let the bullets reign, just like a firing squad each of the men raised their guns and emptied their clips into the four men.

"Let us know if you need us again. I will keep my eyes, ears, and nose to the streets." Jah told Nigel and Malakai.

They nodded and left.

Sorrow

Sorrow looked around Teesha's place and there was so much blood she couldn't see a person getting up from that type of blood loss. So, somebody had to come and move the body. Sorrow believed that she killed Teesha but there was no evidence that Teesha was involved in the kidnapping. Sorrow knew Teesha was still in love with her brother but what would kidnapping their children do to make him love her back. She didn't see the logic in Truth's theory.

Truth kept pacing the floor, "I knew she had something to do with it her confession and the money proved it. My plan was to get the information about the kids. But she just kept talking shit and I held my composure. But, But, when she said Bitch, I had your daughter kidnapped. I lost it. I couldn't control myself." Truth cried.

Sorrow watched her best friend as she popped another pill. She wanted to believe her; Sorrow's thoughts were interrupted by her phone ringing. Ghost. Ignore.
Nigel. Ignore.
Malakai. Ignore. Double fucking ignore. She most definitely didn't want to hear from him unless he was going to tell her why he was fucking Alexus.

She had to keep her mind focused on this dilemma. Every time Sorrow's phone rung Truth jumped and popped another pill. Sorrow snatched the bottle from her and put it in her pocket.

"Are you going to tell Nigel?"

"About what, you popping these pills like candy or the fact that you killed his son's mother?"

"Both."

"Naw, but you will though. If Teesha did have something to do with it, dead women can't talk. And here we are back to square one. We are no closer to finding our kids then we were before you killed her."

Truth broke down in sobs.

Sorrow had no sympathy for her at this moment. She was too closed off to empathy.

She couldn't.

Truth brought this on herself.

"Why didn't you come to one of us?"

"Tsk. Really, Sorrow? Everybody was already treating me like some depressed psycho bitch. So, of course, I set out to do this on my own. That way I had proof that the bitch was involved."

"Like I said before a dead bitch can't tell us shit.

Genesis

Genesis had been everywhere Sabrina would have gone.

The streets say she had been MIA for weeks.

Missing in action.

Gone in the wind.

Sitting in her car it hit her, her mother's house. For days she had watched Sabrina's mom's house. And finally she sees a truck pull up, no one exits the car but the front door creeps open and behold Sabrina comes out in a black wig and sunglasses. Who the hell did she think she was fooling with that shit on? Genesis thought to herself.

Genesis tails them all the way back to Gary. Whoever was in that vehicle with Sabrina was just as clueless as her when it came to street smarts.

Bobbie and Sabrina

"Do you know what the fuck I had to go through? You disappeared and left me with that fucking crazy ass cop. I couldn't even get paid behind your ass." Bobbie screamed in the car.

"Ho, I had to do what I felt was best for my child. You worried about that fucking detective. You need to be worried about Sorrow and them. Especially, if Genesis wakes up, we are some dead bitches."

"Look, I don't give a flying fuck what you do after I get my money. If it was up to me I would have left your ass there, but that crazy mother fucker said you had to be present in order for me to get my bag. For the rest of the trip, I don't want to hear shit from your sheisty ass." Bobbie told Sabrina as she turned her music up.

Good Sabrina thought, Don't nobody want to talk to your confused ass anyway. You a boy mother fucker, not a girl. She would have said it out loud but she needed to get that bag.

Once they hit the sign for Crown Point, Indiana, she turned the music down and threw her cellphone to Sabrina. "Call that mother fucker and ask him where he wants to meet."

Sabrina called the detective. "So, have you found your cousin? My beloved and I are thinking about going to Hawaii with your money." Det. Branson boasted into the phone.

"You and your beloved can get fucked up behind my bag, detective" Sabrina told him.

"Well, Well, if it isn't the neighborhood heartless redheaded bitch. Here I thought your disappearance meant you went to the land of Oz and got a heart." he laughed

"Let's stop with the fuckery Det. Branson. Where do you need us to meet you?"

"Play nice or you won't get shit. The he-she knows where to meet me. Be there in 30 minutes." he commanded

Call ended.

"He said you know where to meet him and we have 30 minutes to get there."

"Fucking dick!" Bobbie was tired of this whole thing. She was not any closer to finding out if Sorrow had something to do with Jason's death. She was not even close to finding out who Black Panther is, this whole thing was a shit storm waiting to happen.

If Sorrow was behind everything the shit the detective was doing to her was payment enough for now. When everything dies down she would be back to kill her ass, if his ass didn't do it first. But, for now, she will get her money and get the fuck out of the G.

Sabrina was thinking the same thing as Bobbie she was going to move to Florida with her money. Because once Sorrow finds out she knew she was going to be dead. She did have second thoughts about what she did to Genesis.

Paying Kameron and his boys to beat her up went too far. She knew how Kameron felt about Genesis. He hated the fact that G was a better man and father than him. She did nothing but love her and make her better. Genesis believed that Sabrina could be a better person. Something she didn't even believe in herself. Fuck it, what's done is done.

"You know what I don't get about your ass, is how in the fuck do you set up the bitch you use to brag about. That girl took care of you and gave you everything. She even took your trifling hoe ass back in, pregnant might I add after you cheated on her and left to be with the nigga. Then on top of that, she's been there for your

95

son since before he was born. Can you tell me why?"

"Man fuck you, Sabrina said and that was all she could say because she didn't know why herself anymore.

Genesis

Their journey ended at Brunswick Library. Genesis witness Sabrina and Bobbie talking to some old white man. "Who in the fuck was this mother fucker?"

Genesis pulled out her cell phone and started snapping photos. She then witnesses the man putting two black gym bags in the back seat. He stuck up his middle finger at them as he hopped in his vehicle. Who should she follow them or him? She had little information on him so she continued to follow the girls.

They ended up what she assumed to be Bobbie's home. She pulled out her cell, "This G, bring me two blizzards."

"What up, G? You mobile."

"Naw, delivery."

She gave him the address and within 30 minutes she was holding two dosages. Genesis was going to wait until she knew they were sleeping. There was no pause before Bobbie opened the door, so there was no alarm.

Wait, Genesis thought, the nigga Jason lived here. These two bitches were connected to Jason's dick in the booty ass. Get the fuck out of here. Genesis had to laugh at herself. She knew that Sabrina was not tied to Jason. But she was tied to Bobbie and Bobbie had to be tied to Jason. Several questions were running around in her brain until it was time for her to make a move.

Genesis went through the garage door that was left open. The suburbs always gave niggas a false sense of security. They felt there was no crime outside of the hood. She pressed the button to garage door closed. Entered the home, shot both with a half of the dosage of the blizzards, tied them to a chair

And waited.

She then looked in the kitchen for food, yes she said to herself as she found the ingredients for stuffed peppers. She hasn't had a decent meal since before the Hospital. She deserved a home-cooked meal. And she deserved it to be at least on one of these bitches' dime.

She boiled the rice.

While she waited. She dragged Sabrina to the dining room and tied her up to the chair. She did the same with Bobbie. She sat them on the sides of the table as if they were ready to enjoy a meal.

She chopped up fresh vegetables. She kept stopping and peering at Sabrina, and the more she held that knife in her hand, the more she had to hold herself back from slitting her throat.

While she waited, She let a tear slip out, How could this Bitch do this to her? Sorrow and Truth told her not to take her back. But, she loved her. And because of that love, it made her betrayal more powerful, it made the hurt cut her deeply.

She wiped her tears and put everything together, baked it and then sat down with a glass of wine and her stuffed peppers. She ate in silence right in front of them, while she waited, staring at both of them with their heads slumped over.

See in order for Genesis not to jump the gun and just kill both of them, she had to keep herself busy. Cooking soothed her. So it was easy for her to have patience. And wait.

Sabrina was the first to stir.

Sabrina

How the fuck did I get tied to the chair? She thought as she started pulling on her restraints; big thick ropes were tied around her legs, hands, and torso. It was cutting into her skin, but she dares not protest because she didn't know who she was protesting against. Or what they were going to do to her.

She kept silent and adjusted her eyes to the dark room. Her head was throbbing so hard she could hear it, but she was able to focus her eyes and the figure in front her was Bobbie. Damn, she was tied up also. What the fuck is going on?

She saw that Bobbie was coming to, "Bobbie, she whispered.

"Unh, why am I tied up Sabrina?" Bobbie said groggily

"I don't know, Bitch, I'm tied up too."

That sobered her up quickly. She tried to make sense of what was going on but her head. Damn, her head hurt.

Sabrina watched as Bobbie squinted her eyes from the pain. "Cuz, maybe if we move our chairs to each other and get our backs together we can untie each other? I am going to move my chair first."

Sabrina moved her chair backwards making a screeching sound against the floor. She gasped as she saw the image sitting at the head of the table, "Fuck me; she said closing her eyes, hoping that the image that she saw was unreal.

She opened her eyes back up.

Still there, but this time a gun was pointed at her Genesis had a glass of wine sitting in front of her, while she puffed on a blunt.

"How does it feel to wake up in hell, my dear?" She said as put the blunt down and sipped on her glass of wine.

"He-hey baby, oh my God I am so glad you are out of that coma. I had no idea my cousin was going to do that, until I came back and saw you lying on the floor, unconscious and bloody. I thought Cameron and I were going to lose you." Tears started streaming down her face.

"Bobbie threatened Cameron's life if I didn't help her and this white cop kidnapped the kids. I know how much you love them G, So, I would have never put them in danger. And she said that she would make sure the white cop tortured the kids on video so I can see."

Sabrina might as well, put it all out there. There was no telling what Genesis saw, she had to be following them. How long? She didn't know the answer to that question. G ignored her.

"Baby, I thought you loved me! Didn't I give you everything a man could have given you besides the flesh of a penis? Tears started to fall from her eyes. How could you do this to me?" Genesis walked up to Sabrina and caresses her face like a long lost lover. She locked eyes with her and read it in her eyes that Genesis loved her and what she did was painful.

"I love you, baby," she told Genesis

"Prove it," she said untying her.

"How?"

Genesis gave her the rest of one of the dosages. "Shoot her with that. Show me where your loyalty lies. Put it in her," she said daringly.

"This bitch lyin-" Bobbie tried to blurt out, but the effects of the blizzard was a little slower to lift up. Sabrina, hurriedly she shot her with the liquid. Instantly, Bobbie became silent.

"Come here baby, Genesis's grabs her on the ass and tongue kisses her with an animalistic hunger.

Genesis kissed Sabrina hard.

Passionately. A raging passion of a killer who was trying their damnedest not to murder their prey too soon, the kiss was an act of prolonging the inevitable.

Violently her tongue assaulted her mouth.

Sabrina tried to match the violence with her tongue passionately.

The drive behind the kisses was different.

Genesis grabbed her pussy, squeezed the fatness with her fingertips, it sent a jolt in Sabrina's body. Sabrina purred.

"Now, untie her and drag her ass to the car. You know I would help you lift a finger in a situation like this but I'm still injured from the kidnapping."

Sabrina smiled, "Ok!" She hurriedly untied her cousin and dragged her to her truck. Genesis grabbed both bags of money, opened them and took pictures of them. She sent the pictures from earlier, the video of Sabrina blaming Bobbie for the kidnapping and the money inside of the black bags.

"It's raining outside", she texted.

"What color?"

"Bullets."

"E.S. my nigga." (Enough said, my nigga)

Genesis put the money in her trunk, then walked back to the garage and got into the back of the truck where Bobbie's body was sitting. Sabrina was in the driver's seat puzzled as to why Genesis chose to sit in the back instead of beside her in the passenger seat. This was not the time to question her actions.

"Where are we going?"

"I will navigate you to our destination, baby."

"Ok, but she was wondering why. Why this and why that?

She instructed her and when she reached their destination, in front of her was believe to be haunting grounds. Grounds that were mentioned subtly in-jokes when Genesis, Sorrow, and Truth got together. The abandoned Steel Mill, where

Sorrow was taught to shoot for the first time and where torture was easily done for the first time.

Painfully Genesis got out the car; she reaches into her pocket and popped a pain pill. She followed behind Sabrina closely, keeping her hand in her pocket concealing her 45. Just in case Bobbie started waking up too soon. Sabrina pulled Bobbie out of the car and dragged her ass through debris until she came to some chains hanging from the ceiling.

"Put the shackles on her and pull the chain to holster her up. I will do the rest." G, held Sabrina close, she put her forehead against Sabrina's and then grabbed her by the neck, "I loved the fuck out of you." She said as she placed the rest of the dosage in her neck. Instantly, she dropped to her knees and fell over.

"Damn, she is about to be heavy, curse me for loving thick girls with my skinny ass."

Chapter 5

Alexus and Malakai

The doorbell rang, Alexus had just started counting her money. She might not have gotten it if Beloved knew what has transpired. She was impatient, she needed and wanted Malakai so bad. She was ashamed to admit Sorrow frightened her. She had shot her own husband, mind you, it was just a tranquilizer gun. But damn what would she have done to her, what will she do to her.   The look in her eyes was murderous, it promised death.

Shaking off the creepy memory of Sorrow, she stuffed the money back into the bag and threw it at the top of her closet. She looked through her peephole a smile spread across her face. Despite Sorrow's warnings, he came back.

He loved her. She hurriedly undid her new locks. Beloved will be mad but, this was why she agreed to do this, it was not for the money it was for love. Alexus opened up the door and Malakai was standing there with a bag and smirk.

Alexus smiled, "You must have gotten the DNA results back?"

"Yeah, I know he is my son. But it's more than that; you were down for me at a vulnerable time in my life. She wasn't riding for me through my prison years. You risked your job and your freedom for me. Plus now you have my son. It's a complete family." he told her as he walked in and sat his bag down.

"What about Sorrow? She's crazy as hell. "

"Don't worry about my wife? We are separated; we live in two different houses, now. But I don't want to talk about her ever. So don't ask me anything about her. I need to handle some business, can I use your laptop?"

"Papi, you don't have to ask to use anything. This is your house now too. I will have my mother bring the children back from her house in Chicago. That way you can meet your son and your step-daughter." She said happily.

"Yo, babe can you cook me something to eat? I'm starving. He said typing away on her computer, looking through her history, checking her email to the date he thought he saw her in Haiti. He did all of that while holding his son's dog tags in his hand. Going through her email, he found what he wanted. Digging further he found an online diary. Beloved this and Beloved that. Malakai this, Malakai that.

The conversations between her and Beloved were coded in her diary. Was Beloved the same white cop that nigga Kameron was talking about? It seemed like Beloved had Alexus brainwashed. He saw Nigel's name in the diary as her daughter's father, but no last name. "Damn, I wonder," he said to himself. He went to the kitchen with his phone.

"Hey beautiful, strike a pose for daddy! I want you to be my screensaver."

"Anything for you Papi!"Alexus smiled and posed for him.

"Gotcha, Damn my baby can be an Instagram model." he sent the picture to Nigel.

He went back into the room and looked into her search history dated back to a month ago. A month ago she was searching for him, Sorrow and Nigel. She came up empty because neither one of them were on social media. So, he went back to her email and bam there was a confirmation for a flight to Haiti. It was made two days before they left. Malakai's phone vibrated, "Sup, cuzzo!"

"How the fuck you know Alexus?"

"Same way you know her."

"Mule and dick service in the joint."

"Yep, he peeked around the corner to make sure she was still cooking. "She claims you got a daughter by her, what you know about that?"

"Unless that jailhouse ho put a hole in the condom, that's not my seed."

112

"Nigga, that's the same thing I was telling Sorrow. A nigga strapped up in that shit but she was supplying the condoms".

"Wait, Sorrow? Is that why she is in a whole other state from you?"

"Naw, she left because she found out I was fucking her."

"Nigga What? MG, I will put a mud hole in your ass for hurting my sister."

"We can go round for round later, but I need you to be at this address tonight. I will text it to you, don't be late and don't tell Sorrow."

"Don't get twisted my nigga we are going to have that conversation sooner or later. It can be later this time since we have dire things to handle. You sitting up there fucking cheating with a ho that everybody in the Indiana state prison system has had and at a time like this. My nigga, where is your head at? I never thought you would be that type of nigga. Anyways, send me a picture of the little girl I can tell by looking at the child if it's mine or not." He ended the call.

Malakai could tell he was heated but being vague about his dealings with Alexus was what it was going to be. Malakai found pictures of the little girl and sent it to Nigel. "Naw they ain't me my nigga. Matter fact, she favors this nigga name Poncho. Did you take a DNA test yet?"

"Yep came out positive he was mine."

"Who took the test?"

"I don't know."

"Think twice about making that claim, my nigga she was a nurse."

Malakai quickly deleted the history on the computer for the last hour. He went through his phone and found the sexy picture he took of

Sorrow while she was lying on her stomach, her sexy chocolate ass was in maroon lace panties, she was poking her ass out looking at him smiling. "Damn, I miss your chocolate ass. Always trying to toot that ass out knowing you didn't have to." He laughed as he rubbed his dick looking at the picture.

He went to the kitchen to find Alexus setting the table.

He came up behind her and pressed his manhood into her ass. "Stop, you said you were hungry. Looks like somebody else is hungry too." she giggled.

"Yep, let me get your phone so I can take this dick pic for you. You remember like you used to do, so you can masturbate to it when I'm not here."

"It's on the table," she told him. She wanted to let him know there were no secrets between them.

Malakai went into the bathroom snapped the dick picture, then he went through her phone and found the number he wanted. He found the number for Beloved.

"Take a look at those dick pictures." He boasted

She laughed, "After we feed you, I will feed him she said pointing to his penis."

He grabbed his bag, I'm going to put this in the closet in our bedroom." he said holding up his bag.

"I told you this your house too, baby."

"Yeah, I know that is why I said "Our" bedroom."

Opening the closet door, sloppily thrown in there was a bag turned over with money hanging out. He snatched one of the bills and saw the mark. I knew it. But, how much does this bitch know?

Alexus

It hit Alexus that she threw the money in the closet. She didn't know rather it landed at the top or if it fell to the floor. She dropped the pot on the table and ran into the bedroom just as Malakai was closing the closet door. "What's wrong baby? Oh, was your other nigga shit in the closet too? You better tell that mother fucker to come get his shit out of my house."

"Yeah right, she opened up the door, the money was concealed but the bag was not zipped. She stepped into the closet and zipped the bag and put it deeper into the closet. "I bought a little something, something for you and I didn't want you to see it until later." she laughed nervously.

"I was just playing. I'm not the snooping type of nigga." He grabbed her by the waist come on and let's go eat so I can give you some of this dick."

"Okay, Papi, she said throwing her voluptuous ass around in her leggings.

Malakai smacked her on her ass hard. It wasn't his wife's ass but it was nice.

"Ouch, she said turning around.

"I'm sorry baby. I just wanted to see if you had hydraulics on that thing."

Alexus was relieved that he didn't see that money. How was she going to explain having that amount of cash? She sat down at the table and he reached his hands out to indicate he wanted to bless the food. She put her hands on his hands, feeling like a Princess in a fairytale. Finally, she had gotten who she wanted. Her family can begin now.

"Heavenly Father, I come to you and I say bless this food I am about to consume. I also ask that you keep my son safe. You know we don't know where he is Lord, but your all-seeing eye does. Let my enemies fall at my feet and die ten horrible deaths for kidnapping my son. May all who are involved parish under your wrath God. Vengeance is mine saith the Lord. I honor that and I honor an eye for an eye."

He squeezes Alexus hands tighter; he felt her hands grow clammy with every utterance of his prayer. He found delight in her uncomfortableness. He felt her fear and so he continued, "Let all that are involved fear you and fear me as you control my hands for the rescue of my child. It's been a little over a month since he was taking. Dear God, let me torture as many as the hours I spent without him reign upon those responsible. Let our bullets reign." Amen

Alexus' heart was beating fast she had felt every word he prayed like volts running through her veins. Each word he uttered was like an electric current of hate. During the rest of dinner, she was silent. But, she pushed that in the back of her mind this was the first time Malakai was able to spend the night with her.

They never had the chance to cuddle after sex. And him staying the night and bringing clothes was the sign that he was telling the truth about him and his wife parting ways. This meant Malakai Gibson was finally hers.

In the beginning, she wanted to the paternity test on both Nigel and Malakai but thought better of it when she found out that they were friends. How would that look to Malakai, she was sure he was not going to be with her if that secret was out. She had made up her mind last night that she would just say that her daughter's father was killed. Fuck Nigel's money, she had Malakai now.

Malakai

Malakai was torn; his mind was tortured, as his thoughts wreaked havoc on his conscious. He would be the boogeyman to one of his sons if he killed Alexus but would be the hero to the other. How can you choose? His thoughts ran rapidly and hindered him incapable to make a decision. He was hoping that prayer would have made her fess up. But it didn't. After talking to Nigel he wasn't even sure the paternity test was legit.

Malakai broke the silence first, "I'm thinking about going to the police. Fuck what my wife says; I think it's time for us to go to the authorities." He said looking up at her facial expression. He saw the glimpse of panic on her face.

"Baby, if it was our son in this situation I would let you do what you needed to do to get him back."

He smiled, "I knew I picked the right one."

He winked at her.

Later that night

Malakai threw on his son's dog tags while he was fucking Alexus from the back anally, he

122

wrapped her hair around his hand several times, and he pulled her head back taking violent strokes. There was no way anyone could confuse these strokes with anything else but anger. He yanked her head so far back that she was looking at her ceiling, he dangled his son's dog tags in her face.

Alexus' eyes widened, she had forgotten about those. Why did she keep those? Dumb ass.

"Where are my son and niece?"

"I honestly don't know baby. I was told a girl was going to drop them off to me and then I dropped them off to this white guy. I really don't know what happened after I handed them over. Please let my hair go." Her head was throbbing.

"Why were you working at my wife's shop?"

"I was just trying to find out where you were and see my competition," she confessed

"Who did you get that bag of money from?"

"The same white guy dropped it off to me at my doorstep two days ago?"

"Is that Beloved? Is that who had something to do with my kids being kidnapped?"

"Yes," she tried to keep calm but his grip was getting tighter by the second.

"What was your part in it? Why were you in Haiti?"

"I was paid to fly to Haiti and break into your car to steal your cell phone. Taking the dog tags was my idea. I wanted to have a piece of you. I walked past that restaurant in the hopes that you would see me and come after me. But you didn't. All I wanted to do was to have you back in my life and for my son to know his father. Please forgive me. All I wanted was you."

"Well, you got your wish, bitch! I found these dog tags right before my wife approached us; you know how long I had to endure your shiesty ass. I would never leave my fucking wife, Ho. Never put a bitch before her, I would never cheat on her. I hated fucking kissing you. It loathed me to have you near my dick." Malakai with one quick motion placed the dog tags around her neck, he pulled back using all his weight.

Alexus

Alexus adrenaline rushed through her as she clawed at Malakai's hands, her nails dug deeply into his hands, kicking her legs around and bucking only seemed to make the strangulation more painful, making his grip more powerful.

In her fight for her life, her children flaring before her eyes. Tears streamed down her face, this was her fate. This is what happens when you are willing to sell your soul to break up a marriage. To get a man.

She felt sleepy and she couldn't concentrate on an escape because there was so much pressure building up in her head. She felt the sting of the chain cutting into her flesh. Where was Beloved now? How stupid of her to think that karma was not going to come back and bite her in the ass. How could she have been a part of the kidnapping of children?

She has children.

All she wanted was a happy family with the man she loved. She couldn't have done it another way. She reasoned with herself. She fucked with this man's child. How could she, when she has children?

126

She has children.

She had children.

Malakai

The dog tags and chain was made out of graphene, a material that would be hard for even an elephant to break. He twisted it, he was losing his grip, it was giving way, and he kept pulling it harder, as he pulled harder. Alexus's head was now lying beside her body. The overflow of blood squirted everywhere. The sheets, the walls, the floor and Malakai's half-naked body were all drenched in blood.

He grabbed her cell and called Beloved, "Did you get your money and your fixed DNA test?" a woman's voice said into the phone he ended the call. The number called back, he texted her back, "Malakai is over here, it was an accident that I called you."

Returned text, Okay, you gave me a scare. Enjoy your new life with Poochie; I will no longer need your services."

Whoever Beloved was she or he knew him personally? Poochie? Because that bitch didn't know him by that name. Who in the fuck were these people? Could it be somebody back in the day, seeking revenge against him and the King Brothers? They killed a lot for C-Note and they didn't give a fuck to know any details about whoever C-Note sent them to kill. They killed Big Bosses, the head of Cartels. He killed and injured a couple niggas in prison. They could be seeking revenge; any one of those niggas could have read his mail from Sorrow. She was the only one that called him that name outside of his family.

Malakai looked at his watch, where the fuck was Nigel?

Nigel

Nigel was walking to his vehicle when he got a call, a three-way call. "If it isn't my two favorite women. It's good to see that you guys patch things up."

The line was silent.

"What's wrong? He held his breath waiting for the worse.

"Nigel. Truth spoke with hesitation and fear, I-I killed Teesha. She had the money with the mark. I swear she did. And I'm not crazy."

He was shocked, not because she was dead shit he wanted her dead plenty of times but he would feel some type of way looking at his son knowing he killed his mother.

He was in shock because he would have never thought Teesha would cross him like that. Or that his wife would kill someone.

Beat Teesha's ass yes, but kill her no. Is she really having a nervous breakdown? Is all of this and the postpartum depression sending her to the edge? The love she had for Nigel Jr. was the reason why she hasn't touched Teesha, although Teesha has tried to provoke her a million times.

Truth never took the bait and stayed classy during the whole ordeal. What Truth was telling him now was the opposite of the woman he married. But there have always been signs that she was no longer the person he had married. She was a shell of her former self, and just before the kidnapping, he had hope because she was showing signs of bringing her old self back. Of course, it was through medication and sessions once a week. But, she was back to being his baby and being a better mother.

The guilt of not understanding the mental state of his wife and the fact that he was distancing himself from her since she spazzed out on Sorrow that night, it started to sink in. He looked at her as a weak link that would get in the way of them finding the children. Before he could make an assumption about her mental state he needed to know what happened.

"Tell me what happened word from word and play by play."

After Truth told him what happened Sorrow confirmed what she saw.

It's some crazy shit going on. Nigel popped his trunk to get his gun out, he walked towards the trunk stopped right there peering at him with hateful accusing eyes. Damn his wife was a murderer.

"You believe me, baby?"

"Hell, yeah baby. I believed you killed her. Cause the bitch body is in my trunk. Let me call Y'all back." He told them as his baby momma looked at him with her dead eyes and a plethora of knife wounds.

A note was stapled to her right breast. "This belongs to you. Any more mishaps the next thing that would be looking up at you is your dead child. I want those drugs from the evidence room stolen and delivered by Thursday, it is now Monday night. Keep fucking with me and I will make sure you or Truth will go to jail. " He left her in his trunk and opted to drive one of the other cars in the garage.

His phone rang, "Do you think she put her in your trunk?"

"Get the fuck out of here! I'm not going to even give an answer to your dumbass question, Sorrow."

"At the rate, shit is going, that's a legitimate ass question. We all know Truth state of mind is fickle right now."

"Look, I know you are questioning your husband's loyalty to you and the shit he is doing. But, I know my fucking wife and she didn't put this bitch in my trunk."

"Hmph, you know your wife, well I knew your wife before she was your fucking wife. And killing someone was never upon her to do list. So, before you try to throw the state of my marriage in my face, Brother. You need to ask yourself, Is the Truth you know the same mother fucker that would kill your baby momma? Yep, I'll wait!"

"Fuck you, Sorrow. I'm standing by mine. And I say she did not put the bitch in my car. End of discussion."

"And you wonder why I went rogue. Because all you mother fuckers are in your feelings. Fuck your feelings, fuck Truth feeling, fuck Malakai feelings and right now fuck my feelings. Feelings aren't going to save our kids. Had your wife but her feelings aside we could be questioning the bitch right now. Instead, we have another problem because of her."

"This coming from the same mother fucker, who let that red-headed bitch disappear. The bitch who holds the key to everything. Miss me with that blame game shit. We all have fucked up. Now, is the time to come together and collect what information we do have. We need to have a meeting tonight. I want to know your plans for the robbery. "

"Yeah, okay." she hung up.

Nigel shook his head and walked towards Malakai's car. "Malakai won't mind if I use his baby," he reasoned especially under the circumstances.

He arrived at what he believed was Alexus house with a bag. The door was unlocked he walked in to find Malakai putting his clothes on, after a much-needed shower.

"What the hell took you so long, nigga?" Malakai looked at his cell, "you are 15 minutes late." he threw him an oversized raincoat, gloves, and three shower caps, one for his head and the other two for his feet.

Nigel set the bag that MG asked for on the table, Malakai grabbed his gloves, "Follow me." Nigel walked into the bedroom. He saw the black bag, he looked in and it was the marked money.

"Come on nigga, Malakai said, grabbing Alexus body.

"Damn, it's the day of the demising baby mamas. Then he saw her severed head, Oh, hell no my nigga. I'm not touching her head." he said grabbing Alexus's legs with his gloved hands. They put her in the bathtub with hot water and bleach. Malakai walked back to retrieve her head. He scrubbed her clean washed her hair, he then wiped down ever part of her house he was in that night.

Nigel washed the sheets while he washed the dishes. They put her body and head right next to the stove. He grabbed his bag and the money bag. Then made sure all windows and doors were shut tight. `Nigel did what he had to do to the stove and to the furnace and he and Malakai walked to their cars. They both drove in the same direction.

When they were five blocks away, they heard and saw the small explosion.

They reached the house in Miller, "My nigga, what the hell was the point of us cleaning her, cleaning the house etc. if you were just going to blow the bitch up."

"Shit, nigga better be safe than sorry."

They parked in the garages, "Is there a reason you are in my baby and what was that comment?"

"Nigga is there a reason as to why you decapitated the bitch. Was her head game really that bad?"

, "Nigga got jokes, Don't worry she wasn't better than your sister."

"Watch your mouth, mother fucker," he said have jokingly.

"The demise of the baby mommas, what was that about?"

Nigel didn't say anything, he just went to the trunk of his car, "See for yourself."

Malakai jumped back a little at seeing Teesha's pale Swiss cheese body. "Who did that shit?"

"Truth."

"Get the fuck out of here." Malakai was stunned.

"I'm thinking maybe I do need to get her some help before this becomes me."

"Naw, Truth must have had a reason and it wasn't your ass. Don't get me wrong she loves your ass but she is not about to kill a bitch over you. What was her reason and how did she end up in your car?" Malakai hated Teesha for obvious reasons.

Nigel told him what she told him.

"I'm thinking about asking her to go to a facility until this all blows over."

"Naw, my nigga. Because, if she did kill her you don't want her talking to a psychiatrist. "By the way, I had a mental breakdown and killed my husband's baby mama." Yeah, that is not going to look good. Her ass would be in jail somewhere. You just need to start keeping your wife close to you." Malakai was giving advice that he needs to start using himself.

Chapter 6

Malakai and Nigel

"White cop? You know how many white cops there are. How many different precincts there are just in the Northwest of Indiana? Shit, we don't even know if it's a Chicago cop?" Malakai said shaking his head.

"We have pissed off a couple of cops back in the day. But, I don't think to the point of where they would kidnap our children. We had our run-ins with the law just like any other criminal." Nigel said

"You know what somebody else has to be involved besides this white cop? Alexus lied and said Beloved was also the white man who gave her the money. When I called the number a woman answered. Then the bitch texted back and referred to me as, Poochie."

"Poochie, that's too close to home. You know cops have all of your fucking nicknames on file. But, everything's coming together we are closer. We just need to touch basis with each other be a unit again. And we need to start with this white cop. Whatever you and my sister got going on, you need to squash that. The same goes for me and

Truth. I already told them and said we need to meet up."

"Are you going to tell Sorrow about Alexus?"

"Naw, we need to stay focused on the facts that will get us closer to finding our children. She was in on it but she couldn't tell me where they are being held."

Nigel got a text, "Not going to be able to make it, something important came up. Need to meet up in a couple of hours." Nigel texts his sister what the note on Teesha said.

"Sorrow said she can't make it."

Malakai just shook his head and went into the house to pour him a drink. Sorrow should know him better than anybody, She said they needed to do everything and anything necessary to find out who kidnapped the kids and that is what he did. Malakai didn't believe in coincidences. And

Alexus, that bitch had too many coincidences in her reappearance in his life.

He was disappointed in Sorrow she was keeping what she was doing under wraps. Just like he was pretty sure she was disappointed in him. But he knew he couldn't push Sorrow into coming back to him, he had to wait for her stubborn ass. But, damn did he miss her.

Chapter 7

Seeing what Genesis sent her, there was
no way in hell she could miss this opportunity to
find out what happened that day the kids were
taken. She was glad that Genesis wasn't around

when she was blaming everybody. In her head, G and Sabrina was the prime suspects.

After making sure Truth was okay Sorrow went home to get all her toys for torture and she wasn't going to stop the torment until somebody told her who had her babies.

In her signature white suit, she pulls down a projector screen. She slowly walks to the machine not making eye contact with her audience, she did not make a sound, and her face was deluded of what she was feeling. They let hope creep into their minds, she did not seem angry. In their heads, the thought of empathy and understanding grew their faith. If her audience would have seen her eyes, just the glimpse of the darkened color her eyes had become, they wouldn't be sitting there with false hope.

If they would have known what her all-white suit represented, they wouldn't have been surprised when she clicked on the machine and spoke, "I don't like to share fear. So, I am going to give you a little glimpse of how I am going to kill you. That way you don't have to fear the unknown, all you have to do is fear ME!" She clicked on the projector and walked back up to the screen with a pointer in her hand.

The first visual popped up, a picture of a man hanging upside down in that very same with chains and there she was with a bat that had a slew of nails and razor blades embedded in the wood.

A smile dangled on her lips, as the tears of recognition gathered up in one of her audience member's eyes. She chuckled, pointing to the bat she was holding, "I remember this just like it was yesterday. I can still hear this bitch as nigga screams bouncing off these very concrete walls. I can still smell his blood lingering in this bat. And I can still smell the fragrance of fatality in this room." She announced as she used the pointer to point to the walls.

She then sniffed the air and smiled, "Can you smell the aroma of his flesh bleeding, dying. Your man! Mmmm, you can never forget the stench of death, especially when it's caused by your hands. And to think the very reason you are in this predicament is because of this dick in the booty ass nigga. So I gather I'm Shakespeare writing a tragedy of Romeo and Mr. Juliet." She laughed in spite of herself and clicked the visual off.

"Well, I guess you are kind of a dick in the booty ass nigga also?" Sorrow laughed

"What?" G asked

"Girl, make her legs do a split and watch that dick come untucked."

"Nah, I'm good I can see his Adam's apple from here." G, now paying attention to Bobbie, he made a pretty ass bitch. Genesis thought as she heated up the poker on top of a garbage fire. She threw the USB along with any other evidence pertaining to that night into the fire also. When the poker was neon orange, she gave it to Sorrow.

Genesis grabbed an ice pick. "Where are the kids?"

Bobbie refused to cooperate after seeing that video. "Fuck you bitches and your kids."

Sorrow took the fire red poker and pressed it against the bottom of Bobbie's feet and then she rolled it down her feet. The skin seared off making a sizzling sound as the skin stuck to the poker. You could hear sheer screams of terror echoing off the walls.

"Where the fuck are the kids?"

Bobbie wanted to say something, a smart remark lead by a pillar of strength in her voice. But, she couldn't the pain weakened her. She was on the verge of passing out, shitting on herself and throwing up from the pain of her flesh being burned and peeled off.

"Maybe we need to change our line of questioning, Gangsta G?

"Yes, I think we do." Genesis put a container of salt and alcohol under Bobbie's feet.

Sorrow again placed the neon red hot poker to her feet, the torment of her flesh being removed from the bottom of her feet. "Oh my God!

Oh my God! Please help me. I promise I will never get involved in something like this again. Take the pain away. She was reasoning with God in her head.

Pulling the chains to lower Bobbie, Bobbie was overjoyed. God was listening to her.

God had granted her mercy.

God had- they stopped lowering her down and placed duct tape over her mouth. Why were they doing that? God, why did they stop lowering me down? The lowering continued, her hope had risen once again, until her feet slowly became engulfed in the mixture of salt and alcohol.

She started bucking; she tried to set herself free from the chains, free from this excruciating pain. The more she tried to get free, the more the chains embedded itself into her skin.

She was now being pulled up, the sigh of relief was captured behind the duct tape. The suffering she has endured made her swallow her pride. It made her tough exterior run away to hide in the corner. She side eyed Sabrina, that bitch was sitting there with not so much as smack or pinch given to her and she was the one who brought her into this bullshit. It was time for her to pay for setting this shit up. It was time for Bobbie to turn on her ass and everybody who was involved.

Sorrow tore off the duct tape. "Do I really need to ask the question again?"

Bobbie was breathless and hoarse when she answered. "I don't know where the kids are. However, that shiesty bitch might, she said gesturing towards Sabrina. She came to me with the kidnapping, her and that fucking detective. I started working at the store to find out if Sorrow had anything to do with Jason or if she was Black Panther. Of course, I was going to kill you if you had. But, I never would have involved anyone's child. The detective had Sabrina come to me with a plan that he could help me get closer to finding Jason's killer if I help him. Plus I would get paid. There were six people who ran up in Genesis house, I was supposed to take your son and the other girl was supposed to take Nigel's daughter. We all had masks on, so I don't know who the other girl was. I had nothing to do with Genesis beat down. Still, in masks, the other girl and I drove the children to a location where a third party was supposed to pick the babies up. That person was Alexus."

Sorrow facial expression was distorted at the mention of Alexus's name. She didn't care if Malakai was knee deep in her pussy, she would shoot through his ass just to kill her.

Focus. Focus. Sorrow couldn't allow her feelings to daydream about how she was going to kill Alexus. She had to focus on what the fuck this bitch was saying.

Focus she willed herself.

"Then Alexus was supposed to hand them over to the detective's wife. But the detective was the only one who contacted us. He is a white detective retired or whatever. He is always talking about his Beloved this, his Beloved that. Which I'm assuming is his wife. I don't know how many people are involved in this bullshit with that racist ass cop."

"What's his name? "

That is when Bobbie became noncompliant. She gave Sabrina a look to warn her not to give out his name either. Bobbie felt that was there only way to get out of this predicament if they withheld the name of the Detective. Her and Sabrina had turned on each other but, they had to do what they had to do together to stay alive.

"Oh, Sorrow laughed, they are on some secret squirrel shit. Okay, let's' do it my way."

Genesis stepped up with the ice pick, grabbed Bobbie's breast and stabbed it, over and over again.

The screams were mortifying as silicon and blood started pouring from her chest. Deflated silicon and breast tissue were hanging out of Bobbie's now mangled breast.

Barely coherent from the pain she managed to say, "You Black Bitch. I should have killed your ass on sight." Bobbie threatened.

Sorrow clutched her imaginary pearls, "No, No, don't insult me, now. She said calmly waving her gun towards her target, I'm not just a Black Bitch, I'm a DEADLY Black Bitch. And you know it breaks my mother fucker heart every time I have to prove this to a man, a Black Man at that."

Sorrow then scratched her head with her gun and continued her speech, "I mean I just don't understand why?"

Genesis laughed, "I know why because those mother fuckers don't live to warn people about it."

"Oh Yeah, that's right," Sorrow chuckled.

Sabrina

Sabrina was mute the whole time. She was not about to speak up for her cousin. It was every grimy bitch for herself. And she wasn't about to be stupid and show any type of loyalty to her cousin. She cringed at the torture antics that was going on beside her. But she felt confident that Genesis had her back.

Genesis loved her.

Worshipped her.

She would not let Sorrow's Sadistic ass hurt her.

She knew she wouldn't.

All this time she had never witnessed or heard about this side of Genesis, she guesses that's why Sorrow called her Gangsta G. This whole thing for her was to break up the bond Genesis and Sorrow had. Then she would be the most important girl in Genesis life. How could she be so stupid?

How could she be so money hungry that she would get herself involved? She can say she did this all for her and Genesis but in reality, Sabrina probably would set up her own mother for money.

"I'm more of a fucking woman than all three of you bitches put together."

"Do you hear the mouth on this one?" Genesis asked Sorrow

"Yes, she has balls."

"Naw, I have balls. You have balls. All this bitch got is a dick."

"You do know just because you have the desire to suck dick, does not make you a fucking woman?" Sorrow laughed

"Oh my, Genesis said now clutching her pearls, now you are using foul language. Tsk, Tsk, What would your husband think, Black Panther?"

Sorrow and Genesis looked at Bobbie for her facial expression. It was priceless, it was one of loathing and hate.

"My apologizes Gangsta G, I guess the shit is fucking contagious." Genesis handed Sorrow her bag and she pulled out a knife and salt.

Bobbie's eyes became like saucers as she watched Genesis walk back over to the fire with the poker. She looked at Sabrina untouched with a smirk on her face. Fuck this shit, fuck family but most of all fuck Sabrina, grimy ass. Family ain't shit.

"Sabrina was the one who came to me with the kidnapping, she was one who left the door open and she is the one who had Kameron and his goons stomp your ass out. She was even going to tell them to pull you off life support." Bobbie let it all out.

"Damnnn, You two are really, really fucking up my torture mood. Before I can get in good with my torturing, she starts talking."

Genesis couldn't lie, she was hurt by hearing that. She wanted to believe Sabrina that it was not her idea. Genesis knew she had to leave the door open, but damn she had Kameron stomp me out. Damn, and the bitch wanted to pull the plug that was given her life. Fuck her feelings and fuck that bitch too.

Anger had not met its most elevated level until now. Genesis was tired of playing with these bitches. She grabbed her gun and emptied every last bullet she had in her clip into the body of Bobbie.

Genesis was about to do the same to Sabrina. Sorrow grabbed the gun, "Naw, not yet!"

Chapter 8

An attractive peanut buttered color black man answered the door, he looked Sorrow up and down with a wide grin. He said nothing, he just ushered her into the building. But he admired the hydraulics her walk gave to her ass.

2 2 was not at all what she envisioned, she pictured some nerdy looking guy. That is what she gets for stereotyping. He took her down some stairs that lead to a room full of electronics that she couldn't identify.

What surprised her the most was the fact that he had a female officer on facetime midst of all his criminal activity.   Sorrow felt uncomfortable with the scowl placed on the officer's face. Could this bitch be trusted? Sorrow opted to be heard and not seen. She moved out of view of the camera on the computer.

Sorrow was not intimidated, but she did not want to have to slice an officer up, her son's life was on the line. She kept her mouth closed, adjusted her wedding ring and raised her eyebrow up.

2 2 saw the knowing look of his police officer friend and the nonverbal exchange between the two women he muted the computer, "Don't worry she's under control. She doesn't know exactly why you are here but she is essential to the information you need to know. I told her you were writing a book dealing with crooked cops and drugs. And Nina is as crooked as they come when it comes to me." he said as he took it off mute.

In the United States, the Drug Enforcement Administration burns illicit drugs such as marijuana, ecstasy, and cocaine at contract facilities. DEA officials transport seized drugs to the incinerator and load them into the device. (DEA agents do not allow the drugs to leave their custody.) If a stash is taking up too much space in DEA storage facilities, a sample might be preserved while the rest is destroyed.

Local law enforcement may use incinerators at hospitals, veterinary clinics, and other facilities. In the case of Northwest Indiana, we use the Steel Mills. Now, am I done being a fucking Wikipedia page for one of your little groupies." she hung up before a rebuttal could be made.

2 2 , chuckled at her antics. "Sorry about that. She really is an asset to me. Anyway, he said as he started tinkering with the computer,

Look, this is the Evidence room database. The evidence filing information he has given you has been scheduled to be discarded in two days. This is the route and the location of the facility. Your best bet is to do the switch in route. Now, the police have become a little creative, by just renting a U-Haul truck and taking it to the facility. Lucky for us this will be sent to the steel mill in Gary. This is the route for them to take they are not supposed to venture from this route. There will be a car with two Swat Team Officers in that car, one in the back and one driving."

"Okay, so basically we need to rent a Uhaul, copy the plates of the U-Haul that the cops will be driving, cause a diversion for the second car to lose sight of the U Haul. Then execute the switch then." Sorrow

"Shit, I like you. You're a fine smart chocolate mother fucker." 2 2 told her.

"Thank you, I need another favor can you give me a visual of the evidence room?"

" No problem, 2 2 said as he punched some other keys to get a visual of the Lake County evidence room."

Sorrow was curious as to why the kidnappers wanted her to break into the evidence room. She thought maybe she could get some clues by looking at all the content that came with this particular drug bust there was nothing that stood out to her. "I need to know who brought that urn in and I want to know who made this bust."

"It's going to take a little time but I can have that for you and I'll call you when I'm done."

"I don't have time to waste."

"Damn, if you weren't married I would have to put you on my team," he told her

Sorrow laughed but was flattered, "It's cute that you think you would even need a team if you had me."

"All jokes aside. Sorry for your situation I'm really glad that I can be a part of bringing someone kids home."

" Don't feel sorry. Don't feel sorry at all just pray for us. But you can feel sorry for the motherfucker who did it."

"Salute," he watched her walk out of his loft, "Damn and salute to that ass," he mumbled.

Chapter 9

Traffic was hectic today with storm clouds hovering over the city of Gary making it look like Gotham City, hauntingly the city grew horrifically dark. The rain was in sync with the splashing of water rolling underneath thousands of tires. The light changed to go at the intersection, a dark blue Bonneville loses control in the middle of the intersection going head-first into black Crown Vic. the hit from the Bonneville stop the Crown Vic in its track pushing it backward making the car behind them rear-end them. the carelessness of the Bonneville calls a four-car pile-up.

The men in the Black Crown Vic trying not to lose sight of the U-Haul yelling on their walkie-talkies that it needs to stop to continue the escort to the destination. After all, they were carrying Precious Cargo. The U-Haul halted under the South Shore train tracks. Just before the highway to get on the skyline. Going slowly down the highway to get off the skyline was a big semi-truck as it slowly cut off the visual that they had of the U-Haul.

Taking the planned opportunity both of the U-Hauls switched places and the drivers also ran to switch places. Now the Haitian drugs were going to be burnt destroyed evidence, and the evidence was now going to be distributed into the community like it was before.

The officer behind the wheel of the U-Haul was a crooked cop paid by C-note. One phone call to him was all that was needed. Sorrow was now behind the wheels of the U-Haul with the evidence in it. She was satisfied that no one would be none the wiser of the switch that just made. She felt she was that much closer to get my children back.

Sorrow knew what she had to do next. but what this be the last thing that the kidnappers have her to do. She did not want to involve Malakai or Nigel. But she needed them.

Sorrow turned to J. Blanco, "I'm not going to be able to show up like I'm Santa Clause and hand keys of drugs over to these niggas without raising any suspicion. I don't know if shit has changed from seven years ago. But I'm sure no illegal Boss is going to go for a present of drugs."

"True that. In order for you to get that type of stupidity is to find you a soldier under that organization that is disloyal and greedy."

Sorrow gave it some thought, "A disloyal mother fucker would take that package and sell the work under the table, underneath his Boss's nose. It's all about his come up. A greedy person would take that package without any questions because they are going to be thinking of all the money they would accumulate. A greedy mother fucker is blinded by its greed."

"You need to present these packages in a familiar way. To save time you are going to have to do the shit at the same time with everybody. Now, that is the problem."

Dropping Blanco off to his vehicle, she held her fist out, "Thanks!"

He grabbed his briefcase and patted it, "Naw, he bumped her fist, thank you!"

He went to pay all of the workers that were involved and had enough money for himself to go on a little vacation. Sorrow also dropped off money to 2 2 for doing his part. She just needed one more favor the identity of whoever did the bust. It was a good thing they retrieved the bags of money from Sabrina and Bobbie because electronic intelligence did not run cheap.

"It's done! Can you meet me at the house? I need Nigel also." bye she hung up the phone.

Chapter 10

Nigel hit ignore on his phone without seeing who it was, Truth was lying by his side with his arm wrapped tightly around her. He smiled at the sight. His smile soon faded as his phone went off again, he finally looked at the number. "Hey, Ms. Williams is Jr. okay?" he asked.

"Yes, he is dear but I have some bad news. Teesha was found stabbed to death."

"Oh my God! What happened? Is Jr. Okay? Do you need me to come get him?"

"The authorities said that it looks as if she was coming this way. I guess to visit. They found her car burned to the ground and her body was just tossed in a deserted house in the woods. They don't know what happened.

Unfortunately, Jr. was eavesdropping and he found out the hard way. I think he needs you."

"Okay, I will come down there tomorrow to see him. Let me speak to him." Nigel's heart broke. This was the part he was dreading. He knew his son would be devastated behind his mom being killed. He braced himself.

"Dad, my mom is gone. I don't know what to do dad. I don't know what to do. How am I going to live without a mommy?" the tears and anguish he heard in his son's voice brought tears to his eyes.

"Little Man, he choked up, you still got me. I'm on my way now. I'm on my way Baby boy."

"No, Dad you have to stay and find my sister."

"What?"

"I heard mommy telling her friend on the phone, that you would never find Semaj. Have you found my sister?"

"No, son. And Please don't repeat those words to anybody. But, Daddy will bring your sister home soon."

"Did mommy die because God didn't like that she wanted my sister gone."

He wanted to say hell, yeah, but instead "No, son your mother would never take your sister away from us, she knows how much you love her."

"Don't worry about me, dad, I like being a big brother so can you please find her?"

"How about I bring you back home and you can help me find her? Do you need me to bring you anything."

"Yes, can you bring me the money you and mom put in my ceiling? I want to make sure I buy mommy lots and lots of flowers."

"Okay, Little Man. love you. I will talk you in a couple of hours." Nigel woke Truth up.

"Did you guys clean the house?"

"Why? Truth said jumping up, did they find the body?"

"Yes, did you guys clean the house."

"Sorrow sent someone."

"Can anybody place you there?"

"No."

"Okay, well put on your face killer it's game time."

"Jr.?" Truth said with tears in her voice.

"He knows." Nigel wanted to tell her about what Jr. overheard. But he felt that she was dealing with too many crises as it is.

"Damn,"

"I have to go pick up some stuff from Teesha's house. Then I'm rolling to go pick him up. Are you going?"

"Yes," she needed to see him, she needed to tell him she was sorry for his pain. The pain that she caused. She was not sure if she did the right thing anymore. How deep was Teesha really in this? She could have just gotten paid for giving out information.

Truth's mind was in turmoil, she had nightmares about that night and her antidepressants wasn't doing anything to help her. She was going to need something harder to cope.

"Okay, I will be back in about 30 minutes."

Nigel entered Teesha's home, it was no sign of murder, they even replaced the table with the same model she had. You could tell the police already searched the house. fingerprint powder was everywhere. They couldn't have found anything because there was no police tape indicating that this was the murder scene.

Nigel went to Jr.'s room and took the money down, he looked through the bag and he could tell right off that money was added to it. Flipping through the money, he saw a stack of 100's with the watermark. "Damn, he cried. I'm glad your dumbass is dead, he screamed into the air. He couldn't stop crying, this stupid bitch has fucked up everybody's life. For what Teesha?

For fucking what? He screamed.

He called Sorrow, "They found the body. Truth was telling the truth I found some of the money in Jr.'s college stash. That bitch had something to do with the kidnapping. If I could I would kill that bitch all over again."

"Damn, I'm sorry Nigel. How is Jr.?"

"Fucked up behind it. But, he's fucked up behind his sister missing also. Yeah, he heard the stupid bitch talking about the kidnapping on the phone to somebody."

Just as he was going through the money a note was stuck in the middle. He read it to himself. "Sorrow, I have to go."

"Nigel wait, I need you and Malakai's help with giving out these packages. I need full access to one of the next Underground Playgrounds events."

"I got you. Call your husband NOW, Sorrow. It's so much you don't even know. Do that for me, Sis?"

"Okay. Tell Jr. I said I love him and to call me."

Chapter 11

A couple of days went by, and each day Thomas Branson would turn on the News.

Nothing. The police department did keep their secrets especially if they feel like it was an inside job.

Phone calls from his fellow men in blue, never mentioned something as dire as the Evidence Room being broken into. He paced back and forth in front of the television cursing with a bottle of Scotch in his hand.

Gulp.

"There is no way in Sam hell, they pulled that heist off without anybody knowing," he mumbled to himself. He specifically told them to break into the evidence room, that way the whole police department would be under scrutiny or humiliated. He wanted the Gary Police Dept. to suffer the same fate of humiliation that he did, they deemed him a failure at his job by making him retire early. He wanted the whole world to recognize them as failures at protecting their own shit.

Beloved rolled her eyes at Thomas, as she watched him gulp down the bottle of Scotch. Beloved saw Thomas as a weak, bitter and pathetic old man.

Nothing more than a pawn.

She smiled to herself but he will never know that she came up behind him and place her arms around his waist, "Babe, there is no reason for you to panic, just give it one more day. If they don't have a suspect yet you know that the break-in will not hit the News just yet. Besides it's just Wednesday, you gave them until Thursday."

He calmed himself for her words soothed him she always knew how to calm the beast in him. She placed a kiss on his lips and walked back out of the room. "Fucking niggers can't do shit right. I can't wait to get rid of the mother fuckers," he mumbled into his bottle of Scotch.

Sorrow

A day had gone and came back again, as she watched the News, and read the Newspaper to see if her plan had worked.

Nothing was mentioned. She was relieved. But knowing the Police Department a fuck up to that magnitude would be kept under wraps. If they caught it before they burned the replacement keys.

She picked up the phone and did a three-way with Truth and Genesis.

"What's Pimping?" Sorrow said

"Me, Truth and Genesis said in unison.

"Bitccccccccccchhhh, Where in the hell have you been?" Truth hollered into the phone when she recognized Genesis' voice.

"Yo, old squeaky ass voice. Damn, Genesis laughed

"How are you? When did you pop your ass back up?"

"I'm good. My eardrum is busted now but other than that I'm healing. I popped up on Sorrow a couple of days ago."

"Oh, so Y'all bitches on some secret squirrel shit." Truth was really hurt that Genesis didn't contact them both.

Sorrow sensing the hurt in Truth's voice reassured her, "It wasn't like that, she contacted me right after your thing. And I felt you had enough on your plate."

"Next time let me. be the judge of that." Truth was tired of everybody telling her what the fuck she could or couldn't handle.

"What thing?" Genesis sensed a lot of tension between her best friends.

"It's not my business to tell." Sorrow said nonchalantly.

"Teesha's funeral is next week. I wonder how they cover up stab wounds."

"Get the fuck out of here. Damn, I know Jr. is fucked up behind that one. Wait a mother fucking minute, True or False?"

"Truth!"

"Damn! Genesis couldn't believe it, Truth was actually telling her she killed Teesha. Truth beating her ass she could believe, but murder her, damn.

"Nigel?"

"Hell Naw! Truth and Sorrow said in unison. As if Truth would kill a bitch over a man.

"Nigel is good, Sorrow said trying to clear up their conversation.

"I'm on my way over there. Truth I suggest your ass do the same."

"I'm not at the house in Miller, I'm in Illinois."

Truth and Genesis arrived at the house. Sorrow stopped them in their tracks. "Before you enter my home, I am telling you what you see and who you see here better not go any further than my doorway. Don't ask me any questions pertaining to what you are about to see."

Going further into the house Truth sees Sorrow's Grandme's, right-hand man. Yeah, Truth thought Sorrow had a lot of secrets to hide. She also saw a couple of her Granmè's Fidelity. When did they fly to the USA? And Why? Sorrow was hiding something and she can guarantee Malakai nor Nigel knows. Because they were supposed to be dead. Genesis didn't know who that big black mother fucker was, so she had no questions to ask.

Sorrow led them down into the basement, to the secret room. Money was stacked up, along with guns and TV monitors.

"Bitch you killed Teesha because of what?" Genesis got right to the point.

"That bitch was in on the kids getting kidnapped."

"Sorry Jr., but she got what she deserved then."

"So, what did she say? Any clues?"

"She said, I'm glad HE didn't want my son. That's it before I attacked her and stabbed her 26 times."

Genesis looked over at Sorrow with a smirk, "like this bitch lying, right?"

"26, bitch!" Sorrow confirmed

"So, it seems like they got the fucking ransom, why do they still have the kids?"

"No, this mother fucker keeps playing with us. This asshole keeps giving us shit to do in order for us to get the kids back." Sorrow brought Genesis up to speed.

"Oh, my God I can't wait to kill this mother fucker. So, the bitch said He. That makes sense an old white dude dropped off the money to Bobbie and Sabrina."

"Have y'all touch basis with the boys?"

"Nope, Sorrow was ashamed to say why she hasn't been speaking to her husband.

"Call them up."

Sorrow went into a safe and pulled out the safe phone and called both of them. 2 2 had hooked her up with a smartphone that disables outside electronics from listening in on your conversations.

"Yo, my niggas," Genesis said happily. Genesis was glad that her friends, her family knew she didn't have anything to do with this bullshit. That is why she will always have loyalty towards them over anybody.

"G, mother fucker glad to see your Gangsta ass is back with us."

"You good, Nigel asked?

"I'm good let's go ahead and put our heads together."

"Kameron and his boys were up at the Underground with the marked money. They were taken care of though. However, they did say that Sabrina paid them to beat your ass. And that Sabrina was dealing with some white cop." Malakai told them.

"Anybody know where Sabrina is?" Nigel questioned

"Tied up, but her cousin Bobbie is dead. They also said a white detective approached them about the kidnapping. They said something about a wife but she might be the one who is just taking care of the kids?"

"They also said that they dropped the baby off to Alexus." Sorrow said matter of fact. Mother fucker sleeping with the fucking enemy.

"Anybody know where Alexus is?"

"Dead," Malakai said, he then continued to tell them what he found on her computer, the plane ticket, Beloved and the white detective. Sorrow showed no expression but she was shocked, maybe she did actually need to sit down and have a conversation with her husband. But that was only if he was the one that killed her.

"So, what we got is an old white man, who may or may not be a cop? Everybody that was linked to it is dead all but three people so far, right?" Genesis was trying to make sense of the situation.

"Yep, Truth told Genesis

"My enemy's enemy is my friend. "Sorrow said aloud.

"What, everyone said together

"This mother fucker rounded up, people who had something against us and paid them to get involved."

"Explain, Malakai said

"Bobbie had something against me because I killed Jason. Sabrina had something against all of us because Genesis put us before her.

Sabrina paid Kameron to beat your ass because he had something against you. Teesha had something against Truth and Nigel because Nigel didn't marry her he married Truth. Alexus wanted me out of the picture to get to Malakai. The old white man has me puzzled. Where does he fit into this shit? And remember we said that the caller had to be white because of the constant racial slurs and certain words he used the kind of indicated he was in law enforcement."

"Yeah, you right! So for sure, we are dealing with a white cop or detective. That shit still doesn't make any sense. Why would he kidnap our children? What is this mother fucker's motive behind this shit? Teesha's wrote a letter stating that it was a White Detective that came to her about the kidnapping? Don't ask me Why the stupid bitch didn't mention his name in the letter?" Nigel chimed in.

"Could be Teesha didn't mention it just in case you found the letter before something happened to her. "Truth said.

A flash of a memory entered Sorrow's mind, the text alert on the safe phone interrupted her flashback. "Truth guess who made the drug bust?" Sorrow showed her the text.

"Who? That old thirsty ass cop she used to fuck around with", Nigel said with laughter.

"Naw, I don't peg that nigga for this. Plus, Officer Duncan is Black." Truth said

"Only way to find out is to contact his ass, baby," Nigel said giving her the go ahead.

"Don't they usually have a whole Drug Task Force Team dealing with drug busts of that magnitude or at least a partner?" questioned Genesis

"You're right!" Sorrow said while texting 2 2 back.

Sorrow's phone kept going off constantly with the information 2 2 was giving her. "He said that for some reason the partner's name is blacked out."

"Damn, who in the fuck blowing up your phone? And who the fuck is he." Malakai asked

Sorrow pushed mute, twisted her lips, looked at Truth as she pointed to the phone and said, "This Nigga!"

"The gall, Truth said twisting her lips.

"Hello, Hello so what you're not going to answer the question?"

"Yes, the mother fucking audacity of this nigga." Sorrow unmuted her phone

Genesis with a puzzled look on her face mouthed, "What the fuck is going on?

Truth just shook her head, indicating that she'll find out later.

"Hello!"

"That there Malakai is my by any means necessary." She said it with no emotion.

There was a void in her voice.

That was not there before.

Not an ounce of anger dripped from her words.

That scared him. It frightened Sorrow, the darkness of her nonchalant attitude seemed so final.

She had distanced herself from him by using his name.

The tone of his name on her lips left puncture wounds in his heart.

His name pronounced with unfamiliarity seemed like an announcement of her exit.

There was silence.

He was silent.

She was silent.

They all were silent.

Death was the cause of such deafening silence.

"Nigga, you asked for that shit?" Nigel said with a chuckle breaking the silence with what he hoped to be a glimmer of hope.

Sorrow didn't laugh.

Malakai kept quiet when the sentence came out of his mouth he knew it was a mistake. However, he is a man. Her man.

He was still her husband.

And she was still his wife.

He hoped.

"Anyways, I retrieved the product, Sorrow said going into the wall pulling out a brick of cocaine. Now, all we have to do is distribute it to the areas he wanted them located in. It's obvious I didn't go according to the plan he laid out for us but I still got the job done."

"What now?" Genesis asked

"I'll get on calling Det. Duncan and finding out what he knows about the dope and the items that were with the dope. And see if he will give me the name of his partner."

"I will get on Sabrina and try to pump out some more information," Genesis said

"I need Nigel and Malakai to set up that meeting at the Underground. We need to get this last quest done so we can get the kids. Either way, whoever is behind this has to die."

"Agreed. For the kids." the team said.

Sorrow hung up the phone with the men. She rubbed the sides of her temples, she was frustrated and exhausted.

"Let's go upstairs!" She said finally

The girls followed Sorrow out of the room and up the stairs. Truth started rummaging through her purse looking for her phone, "Damn, y'all I left my phone in the room."

Genesis shook her head, "You are always misplacing some shit. Damn, where your pussy at? Is it still down there? "Genesis said faking as if she was going to grab her pussy.

Sorrow laughed.

Truth smacked her hand away, laughing herself.

"The code is Gemini's Birthday."

"Ok, she turned around and went back downstairs. Truth hurriedly went into the room opened up the compartment where the cocaine was, she made a little slit in one of the bricks and poured a little into her medicine bottle. She took her phone from out of her back pocket and left out the room.

A smile formed on her face hopefully this will get rid of the flashes in her head of killing Teesha. She had never done cocaine before but she would do anything at this point to ease her mind, even if it was just for one night. She needed to stop her mind from going into that night. She didn't know killing someone even if it was justifiable was this hard psyche. Sorrow had done it many of times, she seemed unbothered. Why was it different for her? Why did these nightmares plague her?

Truth joined the girls with a heavy heart, the guilt of stealing from her friend, her family did not weigh as heavy as the guilt she carried for murdering Teesha. She joked and chilled with her sisters for a couple of hours but in her head, she kept thinking of the little white powder in her medicine bottle.

Her mind wanders in between conversation, What will happen if she partakes in this white powder? Her mother use to do it. It didn't hurt her so why shouldn't she do it to ease these devils, to keep her tormenting memories at bay? This will keep her longing for her child from consuming her into a deeper depression.

On the drive home, she was quiet, Genesis didn't think anything of it because she was too plagued by everything that was happening. She was anxious to get back to Sabrina she needed to find out where her Godchild and niece were? She had no idea her family was going through so much to get them back, she felt guilty for not contacting them sooner. She knew they understood and didn't hold it against her but she felt the guilt.

"Are you going to the beach house in Miller with Nigel?"

"Naw, I'm exhausted just drop me off at home, it's closer."

"Okay" Genesis headed to Truth and Nigel's home.

"See, you tomorrow, Sis. I love you and be safe. "Genesis told her

"Love you too, she told her as she gave her a hug.

"Truth, I can tell you are feeling some type of way about killing Teesha. You should not, I have and will do the same thing for those kids. You shouldn't feel guilty, you did that for your child and ain't shit wrong with that."

"Thank you, for saying that G." she got out the car feeling a little lighter a weight was lifted off her. She needed that she was waiting for her husband or Sorrow to tell her that her killing Teesha was justified. But, they never told her that. However, no one picked up on her turmoil but G.

She got in the house and spread out the lines as they did on TV. She sat back and looked at the white powder she had spread on the table. It's fine 5 lines looked so inviting, ready to satisfy her curiosity, ready to kill her demons and parish her hurt. She got up off the couch and covered the white substance, took two of her antidepressants and got in the shower. She wanted to slumber but it never came, her mind kept going back to that night. It kept recalling the conversation her husband had with their son and the voice of him asking, "What was he supposed to do now without a mother?" That was what was tearing up her heart. The fact that she left her step-son without a mother.

After lying in the bed for hours with no sleep, she decides to go back in the living room where the 5 lines were, the 5 lines that would ease her guilt. The 5 lines that were calling for her to try them.

Shouldn't she?

Or

Should she?

Was she desperate enough for peace that she would alter her mind with this white powder of 5 lines?

Chapter 12

The men were from different areas of Gary and East Chicago, each man was the soldiers of the list of men the cop wanted them to give the dope too. They were all too happy to take the invitation to the Underground Playgrounds. All too many times their bosses would leave the soldiers out of a trip to the Underground. Now it was their time to shine.

The team knew they couldn't let all the men arrive at the same time nor could they have all the men in the same room. Everybody was from different hoods and that meant that they were enemies. They had to plan this carefully if they wanted to succeed.

The seven men came dressed to impress that evening, no white T's or gym shoes. The Underground Playgrounds was a place where class and style was a must. This was Negus entertainment, not Niggas entertainment. No guns, no violence, and no profanity were accepted at the Playgrounds. They were well aware of what the rules were at this elite establishment and the men who made the rules. They were known for enforcing those rules in a very deadly way. They sat the men in different booths, equipped with flat screen televisions, and a woman to their liking, liquor and the finest grade of weed.

These men were used to getting their Bosses and lieutenants scraps they were the worker bees of the drug game. So getting the Boss treatment felt good and now that they had a taste of it, they were willing to do anything to keep getting that high. The women were told to leave the room when the TV came on.

"Gentleman, Nigel spoke with only his silhouette being revealed. My team and I have been watching you very closely and we see your potential in this game. Your skills are underappreciated by your Boss and the other men who rank higher than you. They see you as a bottom feeder you make money for them risking your life to only get a peasant's paycheck for your services. We are willing to give you that come up, there is no catch, no price, just consider us to be Santa Clause and if you do well in this transaction. We will come back and do business with you so you can secure your place as a Boss and take over your territory. If you agree to this then sit back and take a seat. If not then turn the TV off and enjoy the rest of your night on us."

They were watching the men watch the TV screen, not one man turned it off. A smile spread on Nigel's and Malakai's face, they could have let a tear slide down because this meant their children would be coming home.

"I salute you on your journey to becoming your own man. Under your seat is 5 keys of pure cocaine. You can take it from there. Hope to be seeing you real soon." The TV turned off.

Each man looked around like this had to be a joke. Still curious they looked under their seats and pulled out their bags. Unzipped it, 5 bricks were in the bag. This was too good to be true, they assumed it had to be fake cocaine. They tore a piece of the plastic and dipped their fingers in it. Some sampled it on their tongue, two snorted a little. It was the real deal.

They were already calculating they're come up. There was a gun also in the bag, you might have to bump somebody off for your come up. A note said attached to the gun. Each man high tailed it out of there ready to embark on their rise to street stardom.

They hit the streets that night, after the cook up, they were using their clientele that usually cops their Boss's product to sell their work to. The clientele didn't know the difference, but they should have because they kept coming back for more and some never came back.

This was their third rock, they have gotten from their local hood drug dealer, three friends from Portage, Indiana just a mere minutes away decided that they would go to the nearby hood to get crack, they were usually hopped up on cocaine in the powder form but tonight they didn't have much money and needed to get high.

Honestly, they could have gotten high off of their usually Meth dealer in the comforts of their own homes. But they wanted the Black Experience.

Disappointed in the first two the third they decided to go to the dude further down on the next block. This time they would try the soft cocaine that, more expensive but that wanted that Rock Star high. One of the boys gave up his jewelry and his season tickets to the Bulls games. They pulled off buying enough for a couple of friends that wanted to party.

They entered the party like they were Rock Stars, the partygoers knew they were the ones with the coke. They spread the lines on the table, they were experts at this, it was 16 lines on the table. All who wanted a line or two held they're rolled up dollar bills.

"Let's do this shit at the same time!" one party goer said.

They all leaned in to get their hit of coke, "Ready? Set, Go, they all snorted and leaned their hands back at the same time.

Feeling the drug, something was wrong, something was wrong with all of them, some fell down in convulsions, others were vomiting. Then most of them passed out on the floor not moving.

Seeing this event take place some partygoers ran out the house, while girls started screaming getting on their cell phones and calling the authorities but not before they posted pictures on their Instagram and Facebook pages. Not before they tweeted the situation on Twitter.

Not before some of their friends died over tainted drugs only meant to kill those with darker skin than theirs, or poorer homes, or lessor schooling.

And this incident is the one that hit the news the most, the white kids who decided to risk their lives by going into a black neighborhood only to buy coke for their friends. It sounds innocent doesn't it, poor little rich white children at the wrong place at the wrong time.

16 dead!

16 white kids dead!

An outrage!

Det. Branson got a call to be informed about his three nephews dying from a drug overdose. His sister would be devastated but if 16 whites were affected then he knew that the toll on black lives was going to be 5 times greater than them. He didn't give a fuck, they liked rap music and wore black drug dealer's attire. So, they needed to be killed, he wanted the world to be pure white. No, Nigger lovers allowed either.

Chapter 13

Malakai had awoken from a restless sleep once again without his wife by his side, he vowed that this was going to be the last night without his wife by his side. Grabbing his coffee, his remote, he sat down as he always had done and turned on the News.

The News was panicked by the overnight chaos of death. Death had plagued the hood once again but this time, this was genocide of a magnitude that could become greater than the years that Gary, Indiana was the murder per Capita of the world. And that took a whole year this was just overnight.

Breaking News

In the last 72 hours, mostly the Gary area and surrounding cities have reported numerous of deaths from end-organ damage, reports of darkened lesions upon the skin to irregular heart beat to death. And all these incidents have been linked to the cocaine found in patients systems. Cocaine laced with high quantities of Levamisole and Fentanyl. When the victims were tested 50% of the cocaine were tainted with Levamisole and Fentanyl.

In a single-center review of cases, most patients who'd taken the adulterated cocaine tainted with Levamisole not only had darkened skin lesions caused by blocked blood flow, but also had some form of end-organ damage, including blood in the urine and elevated liver enzymes, which are signs of cocaine being tainted with the drug Levamisole.

In some patients, there are also signs of cocaine tainted with Fentanyl. We are told when Fentanyl is combined with other drugs like cocaine or heroin or used by itself in high doses it causes your heart to become unbalanced and it starts beating irregular. Breathing can become extremely difficult to the point that it's almost impossible to breathe at all. Death is right around the corner.

Researchers suspect it's a favored adulterant because it can increase dopaminergic responses to cocaine and is also metabolized into an amphetamine-like byproduct, boosting the drug's effects. Also, it blends well and is stable in the crack formulation of the drug.

In 2005, Fentanyl and Levamisole were found in almost 2 percent of the cocaine seized by the DEA. In 2007, the frequency went up to 15 *percent, and by 2011 a staggering 73 percent of all cocaine seized by the DEA had been cut with Fentanyl or Levamisole or sometimes the combination of the two.*

Lake County DEA seized a large shipment of Fentanyl and Levamisole tainted cocaine in 2011 before it hit the streets. Our sources say that this is the same chemical makeup of that batch of cocaine. And if this is true someone in the Lake County DEA has dropped the ball.

Citizens of Lake County demands to know how could a product seized six years ago plague their cities today. There are not only rumors of deadly tainted drugs being unleashed but a tainted Police department who unleashed it. There are no comments at this time from the authorities. This has left 50 dead, 92 hospitalized on their deathbeds and we are told there are more being reported by the droves.

Malakai dialed Sorrow, "You see this shit, So!"

"Yep, I will be there in 30 minutes," she told him. Nigel was already at the Miller Beach house.

"What in the hell is going on?"

"Let me see that map, Sorrow said coming down the stairs. The way 2 2 said it's coming over on the police radio, these are all the sections that the deaths are occurring. These are the neighborhoods they are finding to be affected. They either live around or they finding them some just lying in the streets dead. They found people dead in cars on their way to the hospital. He said the news is lying about the death toll, it is greater. They just haven't found them yet."

"Damn, that mother fucker set us up to kill our own people. Pure genocide." Malakai shook his head.

Nigel ran his hands over his face, "This is fucked up. And I feel bad about it but we need to get our children back. If this mother fucker is capable of this, what in the hell is he capable of doing to two little black kids he is holding hostage?"

"You right!"

"What's done is done? I'm sorry about the shit and the lives of all my brother and sisters. But we need to find ours before he does something." he said, hugging his wife.

She embraced him and kissed him, he knew that he had a couple of relatives and friends that do drugs. Dope dealers that use to be as big as them now succumbed to this drug shit and now it was no longer a slow death. They had unknowingly put something more deadly out in the streets.

"How can we fix this? Sorrow said pacing back a forward. I should have known. This was why he was so specific in his details of how he wanted it done. I should have known something was up, but how would I know that this was going to be a situation of this proportion." Sorrow was still in her feelings, yes she wanted her child back and this was there by any means necessary.

"Sorrow, this shit right here cannot be fixed, we can't put the dude out there because we have to find our kids. He has us stuck and he knows it. Besides we gave it to the dealers, we stole the U-Haul, I mean this is all on us, right now in the eyes of the law."

"It was a good thing we didn't show our faces to those dealers. I have to call Roc and Bone to set shit straight with them. Those little niggas might implicate their business. We have to kill the cop you used."

"I'll make the call." She texted Blanco, all eyes are what she text and bam the crooked police Officer would be dead within an hour.

"Has anyone been called?"

"Nope, I haven't gotten a text either."

"This mother fucker playing still, Malakai screamed.

"We need to be patient and I know at this time you all don't want to hear this, but we need to go back in these streets and find out who in the fuck this white detective is and Now." Sorrow said

"Yeah, let me catch up with my wife to see if she talked to Duncan?" He called no answer.

Malakai pulled Sorrow off to the side.

"Baby, you okay? Malakai asked.

Sorrow has not said anything about Alexus once she found out he killed her. She knew what it was and that was all the confirmation she needed to go on with her marriage. There was no love there.

I know people might think it's crazy, yes she saw him fuck another woman, had a whole fake relationship with her so he can get close to her because she had something to do with the kids

217

getting kidnap. It might have been another way, but he didn't have any other way than that. Women stayed with men who did more than that to them. "I love you, she told him.

"If you look on the tapes, baby. I had anal sex with the bitch once and she sucked me off twice. And that's only because the bitch kept on asking why I wasn't sexual with her-"

Sorrow cut him off, "I don't need to know what you did. I just wanted to know why you did it. And I know now, so I will get over it. But, don't let this shit happen again without you telling me the truth upfront. I don't want to have to shoot your ass again."

"Her son is not mine either, she faked the DNA test. I read it in one of her text messages."

"Even, if it was I know that it happened when we weren't together. I would have embraced him if he was yours period."

And just like that, they were back. But their focus was not on them it was on finding who the hell the detective was and getting the kids home.

Bullets Reign

While Malakai and his sister were talking, he called Roc.

"You know where they are?"

"Yep,

"Well, then let the bullets reign." Roc Vega said and hung up.

Nigel did not like the fact that they had to kill some young boys. Back in the day, he wouldn't give this type of shit a second thought. Now, his mentality was different. He knew what needed to be done and he was going to make sure the situation gets dealt with, but it doesn't mean he couldn't feel some type of way about.

Sorrow knew her brother was at odds with killing those boys, they all were. Especially since the death toll was climbing to more than 150 with their help. It was their fault they were in this situation. Sorrow went over and placed

her hand on Nigel's shoulder, "For the children.
"

"For the children, Nigel repeated getting
his head back into the game.

"Let the bullets reign." Sorrow said as
everybody stepped out to get their gear together,
vest and all. They would never underestimate the
streets of Gary. These Gary streets were lethal
and they should know they were born and breed
into this shit. This time they were going in it
together.

No rogue shit. No, I will do it myself shit.
They were a team on a mission that would leave
their city streets in a rain of bullets. They
knew going into an unknown situation with little
time to prepare could lead to one or all of their
deaths. They had planned for their deaths years
ago. But, they had been blessed thus far. Who is
to say their blessings haven't run out?

Chapter 14

The first neighborhood they had to wait for a minute, they scoped it out and watched as the dope house handled business. No one was standing outside selling dope in this neighborhood. They were hoping to catch the dude coming or going, they were not that lucky. The streets of G.I. were dark, the creatures of the night were on a hiatus from the streets, some were just given death by the streets.

Genesis looked at Sorrow, she gave her a look they would have to wing it going into the dope house and do what they had to and if that meant more casualties then so be it. They then went to the other spots.

"There he goes right there, Nigel said. As they watched a young dude in flashy gear serve dope, there were three others not that far from him.

"Drive by?" Nigel suggested

"Drive by, they all agreed.

They turned up their music and made sure their lights were on, everybody knew the signs of death by drive-by were lights off, and quietness. They did just the opposite. Malakai leaned down, a man and two females were most likely not to kill his ass then two niggas and two females. They had to give him a false sense of safety or he wouldn't come close to the car.

"Ah, Bob bring yo big ass head here my nigga! Nigel said hollering out the car. Bob tried to peer in the car, he saw a nigga and two bitches. The voice sounded familiar but he couldn't see the face, so he stood where he was at, he wasn't going to the car.

"Who that?" he hollered back. The other men didn't give it any thought because whoever was in the car knew his name.

"Nigga, I heard yo ass was up in the Underground-Nigel didn't need to say anymore. Bob started walking towards the vehicle not wanting the others to hear.

When he was within arms reach, Malakai lifted up in the back seat of the passenger side, before he knew what was happening Malakai shot him in the head twice. Before Bob's body hit the ground they sped off with bullets barely hitting their back bumper.

"One down, "

"Too many to go," Nigel said

The other area was a ghost town, there wasn't anyone out not even the smokers that were left. "What now?" Nigel said.

"Let me call 2, to give us all of the addresses. That way if we run into this problem again we are just going to have to take care of them, niggas, where they lay their heads at. The streets are hot right now, so I know the smarts ones are probably keeping a low profile."

"Yo, text me those addresses of those names I asked for earlier."

A minute later, her phone was chiming off back to back.

"This the address, Sorrow said pulling up.

"Ain't this the same place we gave the little nigga the invite at? Malakai, shook his head, man these young mother fuckers just don't give a fuck. He's selling in front of his own house. "

"Whatever, I know plenty of niggas back in y'all era that did the same shit." Genesis pointed out

In unison, "But they weren't taught the C-note way!"

"All bullshit aside, who live with him?"

"Don't know. Crackhead time, come on G, Sorrow said getting out the car.

"You use to be a Prom Queen, now you just a Crack fiend!"

"Bitch, you got jokes, You smoking the same shit I am. Mother fucking yella bitches get on my fuckin nerves." Sorrow said loudly

"Fuck ya black ass, crack heads comb their hair now a day this ain't the fucking 80's. "

They kept the commotion going on as they stopped in front of the house.

"They take baths too, but I don't see ya dirty ass fiending for no fucking soap. Got me out here talking about we got that good shit in my hood. WHERE THE FUCK IS THE GOOD SHIT AT THEN, COOKIE? I don't even see the dope boys in this mother fucker."

"We tried yo hood, bitch. Wack ass dope sold by some wack ass niggas." Genesis got even louder, "These niggas know me up in here. I been smoking dope since 1994 with these niggas." She did the cabbage patch as she hollered, "FUCK WIT ME! FUCK WIT ME DJAY!"

"That played out shit, Bitch watch me Twerk, and Sorrow starts to twerk.

"Bitch you twerking for crack. Ah, I ain't mad at chu. Genesis started twerking and chanting, "We twerking for some crack. Twerking for some crack." Sorrow started singing along also.

The dude peeped the crackhead shenanigans outside. "I know good and fucking well these hoes ain't arguing in front of my fucking spot." He needed to get out there before they drew any more attention to themselves and somebody called the people.

Nigel was cracking up and Malakai was laughing his ass in the car. But Malakai loved the way his wife was twerking that ass. They watched as the dude came out the house and all laughing stopped.

"Yo, he screamed at them coming down the walkway, Y'all need to move the fuck-

Sorrow and Genesis pulled out and lit his body up. They hopped their asses in the car and was on to the next one.

Genesis was rolling, "Bitch did you say yo ass need to be fiending for some soap. I'm dead." She said reloading their guns.

Sorrow laughed, Naw, this ain't the 80's bitch that was funny."

They calmed down when they saw that Nigel was all business, "Who next?"

"This dude's home address is up the street actually." Sorrow said.

" How the fuck y'all quoting movie lines and doing the cabbage patch. Then Panther's retarded ass out there twerking for crack. You two need to be on YouTube some damn where." Nigel laughed

"Where in the fuck did you get the name Cookie from?" Genesis laughed

"Her ass was watching Empire before y'all showed up. The name Cookie was stuck in her head." Malakai laughed

They laughed, the house was dark and it wasn't but two houses on the block an abandoned one and the dudes. Across the street was a wooded area. They could see the small pile of mail but a glow from a TV was still on.

"I'll go!" Nigel said getting out the car with his hand on his gun. He tried the knob, he then went to the side windows to peep in, somebody was on the couch sleep. He went to the back, broke the glass window out to reach the knob, he was in, Nigel pulled his gun out and walked in the direction where he saw the dude sleeping.

He saw dope in lines on the table, a rolled up dollar bill on the nigga's lap. He nudged him, "Wakey, Wakey!" No response. He then checked his pulse there was none. He bagged his way out of the house.

He jumped in the car, "That dope got that nigga. Who's next?"

"That one nigga snort too, the Spanish cat from EC, look his name up, right quick. Malakai said

"Damn, that nigga dead too behind that shit."

They drove to the next it was a slew of men beating one man down. Then another man got out of the care the other men parted like the Red Sea. The man shot the one beaten down several times. "Let, that be a fucking lesson to the rest of you mother fuckers. Never cross Smoke." Everybody got out of dodge even the dude Smoke sped away in the car.

A neighbor ran out the house with her phone, calling the Police Malakai got out of the car. He was talking to the neighbor and he came back to the car, "And then there were two." He said shutting the door

"They must have found out that nigga was selling his own shit."

"I don't miss this shit not one bit," Nigel said

They pulled up on the next one.

"Mother Fucker, you don't do shit for yo son."

"Get the fuck off my block with that shit, Nikki."

"Fuck you! I go where the fuck I want to."

"How in the fuck you bringing my son to the spot this time of night? Man, get the fuck on wit dat shit bitch." Tim told her trying to walk away

"Because nigga he needs shit and you out here with money. So give me some money." She said as she tried to reach into his pockets.

Tim reached back and punched her dead in her eye.

"Damn, that's fucked up", Gen said

They heard the baby start screaming as his mother was holding her eye ashamed and crying.

She pulled out her cell phone, "I'mma bout to get your ass locked the fuck up, you fuck boy."

He smacked her cell phone out of her hand, grabbed her by her hair and started smacking her with the back of his hand repeatedly.

"Don'tcha trifling ass eva threaten me with the police. Now, bitch I said- Nigel ran up on him and shot his ass up. Went into his pockets, found a wad of cash and threw it to the girl.

Nigel had a mask over his mouth, "Now, have some respect for yourself and your son. Don't be out here begging a nigga to do what he is supposed to do. And don't let a mother fucker beat your ass either." Nigel was disgusted.

"Let's hurry up and get this last one done, these new breeds of niggas getting on my fucking nerves."

They pulled over to the side of the road and suited up with masks, body armor, ammo, and guns. From the look of their first encounter with this trap house, it housed a lot of drug dealers and they kept going in and out. Everybody except for G was suited they sent her inside in her regular clothes.

"Where Tyrell?" G said to the nigga who eyes popped out of his head at her cleavage.

"Dat nigga in the kitchen." He points towards that way, he watched her slim thick ass walk all the way to the kitchen.

"What's up, Rell?"

"Damn, What up? Who you?" He said licking his lips

G blushed and stepped forward, "I can- be who you want me to be later. But, right now Daddy, I came for that gas. "

He smiled, as he went to the draw to get to his stash. "Whatcha looking for Queen?

"Quarter."

"Oh, that nigga must have given you a little change to spend."

"Naw, I gets my own coins and if it was a nigga sponsoring me, that nigga better come with more than some fucking quarter money. "

"Is that right, he said walking up on her.

She let him get close enough to kiss her, she put her two fingers in the middle of her breast and pulled out his money, "Later, she said smiling at him.

"Most def later." As he went to his stash, he was showing off counting his money with his back towards her. She shook her head as she took the opportunity to unlock the back door. She went back to the spot she was in, "Well, let me get out of here I got my girls in the car."

"Are the fine too?"

"Birds of a feather, baby"

"Come through with them too, later."

"Maybe sooner, maybe a lot sooner,"

.

He walked her to the door and she got back into the car. They pulled off and parked down the street.

"5 niggas, no upstairs, no basement, the backdoor is unlocked so we have to move fast before they realize it is locked. I'm sure all of them could be toting guns, but I am not sure. I know the dude that answered the door is, it's a dark-skinned bald dude in red he has one. It's a couple of guns sitting on the floor in front of them and dude Tyrell has one in his pants leg. And the weed is in the kitchen in the draw"

"Weed? Why are we discussing weed?" MG asked

Sorrow chuckled because she already knew what G was about to say.

Genesis pulled out her quarter and smelled it, "Cause that nigga got some high-quality gas. Duh, mother fucker. This nigga!" G said pointing at Malakai

"Gear up, so our low level asses can rob these mother fuckers for some weed. "

"Oh, so I'm low level. I bet your ass is going to want to smoke some of this low-level bitch's shit." She told Nigel

He didn't say anything he just got out the car laughing. They headed for the back door, G peeked in the side window and saw all of them in the living room watching Martin and getting high.

"Living Room." They crept to the back door opening it slowly, they stood in the kitchen ready. They had the TV up so loud they wouldn't have even heard the Police knocking. G peeked around the corner and saw Tyrell standing up between the kitchen and living room entryway.

Genesis nodded, MG, Nigel and she walked backward into the middle of the kitchen with their guns aimed and ready. Sorrow hit the light switch put her gun to Tyrell's head, and watched as the bullets whizzed through his head, leaving a spray of blood on her face. Sorrow leaped backwards further into the kitchen out of the way with her gun aimed. He dropped to the floor as his boys leaped up with their guns, running straight into a death trap.

Nigel, Malakai, and Genesis instantly started shooting and watched their bodies shake with each hit of the bullets, blood, gunfire, and shells were flying everywhere. They killed every last one of them in a rain of bullets.

Everybody was dead, G grabbed her weed and they headed out.

It was over!

Well, at least that part was.

It was 4am in the morning when they finally finished everyone off. Nigel called his wife again to see if she would answer. Still no answer, he would just go home tomorrow to see what is up. Usually, if she takes a Xanax she would be out for a while.

Chapter 15

Truth opened her eyes, her surroundings were stark white, and she was delighted that it was not a dark blood red. She felt a sense of wellbeing. She placed her feet on the floor and felt the softness of it. She rubbed her bare feet across it, liking the feeling of padding against her feet. She looked around and the walls looked to be the same material.

"Why were the floor and walls padded?" She asked herself. Truth tried touching the walls but she couldn't move her hands, they were tied crisscrossed around her sides, she wiggled she couldn't move. Panic arrived as she looked down and saw she was wearing a straightjacket.

She threw herself against the walls and she bounced back a little but she felt the softness of the wall. Panic drove her to tears, was she in an insane asylum? Only insane asylums had padded rooms. She ran to the door and peered out the small window, women in white old time nurses' uniforms walked the hall with a clipboard in one head and small child in the other. All of them, why were all of them holding a child. She threw her body against the door making a noise, at the same time all the nurses turned around wearing Teesha's bloody face and the small child had the face of her daughter, she started walking backwards in disbelieve. She chanted, "Wake up! Wake up!"

The door to her padded room opened and one by one each nurse came in and slits started to appear on their skins, they poured blood out.She counted them there were 26 Teesha nurses each holding her child.

The little girls started crying at the same time, "Bad mommy, look at what you did to my Brother's mom."

Truth woke up in a cold sweat, sitting up making sure she could move her arms. She looked around she was at home. Her heart was still racing from the nightmare. She was at her wit's end with this bullshit. She didn't want to spend another night conscious in her nightmares. She wanted to crash, and dream of tea parties, dress up and chasing rainbows all with her daughter.

She looked at the 5 lines on the table and said fuck it. But, how many was she supposed to do for her first time? Who in the hell would she call to answer that question? She was scared at first rolling up one of the 50's she had in her purse. Damn, she didn't want her nose to start bleeding, she put the rolled of 50 down. She shook her head that was just on TV, this little bit wouldn't make her nose bleed. Her cell phone went off, Det. Duncan texted her and was asking were they still on for coffee?

She texted back, "Yeah. It's very important. Like I said it's some legal mess I might have gotten into, with a bad guy. That you might know."

"For sure, he said, but make sure you are on time because it's major shit that went down overnight. But, if it's life and death I will meet you."

"It is life and death."

"Sure, don't be late. I know you pride yourself on being prompt."

"Things have not changed."

She looked at the time she had about an hour to meet him, she didn't even realize that it was 9 am. She had several calls from her husband. But, yet she spent another night alone. She can't fault Nigel; she knows Nigel will have straight tunnel vision when he is faced with a big problem. The only thing that mattered to him right now was finding his daughter and nephew. But, him not being at home still made her feel neglected and unwanted.

Truth put the opening of the rolled up 50 up her nose, she placed the other end on top of the coke, and she held one nostril and snorted the white powder up her nose. She jumped up, "OMG it burns, she started coughing and she remembers the first time she caught her mom doing coke. Her mom had tilted her head back, pinched her nose and swallowed.

Truth did the same, she heard her heartbeat quicken, she started sweating, she felt dizzy and she started vomiting. She couldn't feel her legs, she was panicking, her eyes were dotting back and forth and her heart started to ache. Truth tried to stand and she hit the floor, her phone was ringing when she became incoherent.

Det. Duncan decided to use his authority to find out where Truth's cellphone was located. It was not like Truth to be late and she was 30 minutes late.

She answered her phone but there was silence on the other end so he stayed on the line. When it was traced he sped over there, she said she was involved with some bad man. It was not a flame still brewing for her, he felt like it was his duty to make sure she was okay. And he was a detective now his mindset was different than it was 7 or 8 years ago when he was using his badge to get pussy.

Duncan was surprised when he reached Truth's neighborhood, not that she wouldn't be in a neighborhood like this, but that she would still be living in Gary. Truth was always a little money hungry.

When he drove through these types of neighborhoods in Gary, it brought him pride. He arrived at the King's abode. He just couldn't believe Truth would be living in the hood. But, this type of neighborhood, with well-manicured lawns, and big houses was right up her alley.

Damn, this was a nice house, like a miniature mansion He knocked on her door, to find it adjacent, "Truth, he called before he opened the door any more than it already was.

He tried to open it more and step in but something was stopping him, he peeked around the corner to find Truth lying on the floor right behind the door He quickly checked her breathing, checked her pulse very faint, he tried smacking her awake, her eyes barely fluttered from the pain. He happened to look over at the table, he ran over there to get a better look. He was puzzled he sees a lot has changed over the years he never thought that she would become a user.

It was four lines left on the table; there was no way for him to guess how many lines she has snorted. But if this was the tainted cocaine that was going around he better get his Narcan out the car.

Running to his car, he saw a truck pull up in the driveway, he didn't pay it any attention, he needed to help Truth and now. He grabbed it and got back out running, only to be greeted with a nine to his chest.

"Who in the fuck are you? Where is my wife?"

"Look I'm Det. Duncan, he slowly went for his badge, if your wife is Truth Blazi-"

"Truth King Mother fucker."

"Mr. King, I'm an old friend, we were supposed to meet, she didn't show, I GPS her, and I found her passed out."

Nigel ran with the Duncan on his heels Duncan hit the floor and injected her with the overdose blocker. "What the hell did you just inject her with?"

"It's an overdose blocker"

"Overdose Blocker?" Nigel was confused since when was Truth using street drugs

He saw the disbelieve on Truth's husband's face, "That was on the table when I got here. He said pointing to the table.

Nigel walked over to the table, what the fuck? Where in the fuck would she get −"Yo we have to get her to the Hospital. She took some tainted drugs." Nigel said grabbing his wife.

"I can call it in and get an ambulance here in no −"

"Naw, my nigga we not doing it that way. And on the ride to the hospital, I need you to tell us who was on the drug bust with you when you got the tainted drugs in the evidence room." Nigel held Truth in his arms riding in the back of Duncan's car.

He was puzzled over the question and how did he know he was on that bust with his partner. Det. Duncan started ranting, "Mother fucker, that white racist mother fucker actually did it. Det. Thomas Branson did this shit. He joked about how he could spread that shit to the blacks and damn near the whole city of Gary would be dead. Because in his head blacks were all on drugs and criminals. I told them mother fuckers he was not joking, that is why I asked him to be removed from my drug squad because of his racist comments and acts.

After that, a lot of cops decided to let our Superiors know about his conduct and they made him retire a week later. He threatened everyone in the precinct, especially every black, his exact words were, "Don't be surprised when you monkeys get ready for that first hit of crack it will be your last. Render your asses back into slavery."

"Detective Branson, that racist ass mother fucking Branson," Nigel said to himself. He looked down at his wife

"Look, man, this whole incident is off the records but my superiors need to know where this is coming from and how did they get a whole of it?"

"My little cousin said this old white dude kept coming around saying he got a hold of some good shit. But, one of the older boys he worked for was like that nigga a detective that use to work with Det. Duncan, don't trust him. But, said the dude kept coming around, blackmailing him, making him look bad by talking to a cop. He told him he would do it, just to get rid of him. Lil cuz said he came to him with keys of the shit, said he didn't want anything back for it, if he didn't sell it he was going to use his connections in the Police Department to have everybody out on the block with him arrested and make it seem as if he was a police informant. So, he called us and I told him don't do the shit. And we told him to bring a little sample to my house. Truth said she knew you but she didn't know who your partner was. Next thing I know he called panicking said some niggas came in with ski masks and guns and took the shit. I thought the little nigga was lying at first but when he started crying about the detective coming for him. He couldn't give me the dude name so that's when I ask her to call you up to see if when can do something about it on the hush, without involving my little cousin."

"How did you hear about the dope being tainted?'

"That shit is all over the internet, Facebook, the News. I came home to ask Truth did she hear about it and you know the rest. I just can't for the life of me, figure out why my wife decided to do some fucking drugs?" he said puzzled.

Duncan was happy to know Truth wasn't a user, he didn't know what made her curious about the shit. He finally made it to the Hospital; Nigel opened the door and carried her out while Duncan told the ER that he had someone who was given a laced cigarette with the tainted cocaine. Nigel was grateful.

Duncan grabbed Nigel's shoulder and looked him in the eye, "This situation never happened, I informed the staff that she was drugged with a tainted cigarette." Duncan figured out in the car who Nigel was, he remembered many of pictures of him and his brother in the back offices of the Police Dept. Detective Branson had a hard-on for the King Brothers and anybody associated with them.

He did scrupulous acts to entrap a witness and doctored up some paperwork to arrest Malakai for the murders. He tried to do the same thing in the Duke Cash case and was mad when Nigel came out of hiding and people started digging through the evidence for Malakai on the Chicago murders. That case was dismissed.

Nigel did a couple of years but that case was dismissed. He knew that Branson took them through all of that, but it would be wrong for him to give out information about Thomas knowing that because Truth has been affected by these drugs that Nigel was going to go, after Thomas. It was a wrong and a right way to get justice.

Duncan knew the department forced Det. Branson into early retirement because his cases kept getting dismissed not because he was a fucking racist. The timing just fell into place with public slurs of hate for minorities coming from his lips. Lake County's way to keep the black majority precinct happy. We were the only ones that didn't give a fuck about venturing into Gary.

He hated that mother fucker, so he would take a page from his book and go through a couple of loopholes to get his ass. Despite what people think all blacks don't bleed for blue because we are cops. We still bleed for black but only if you were in the right.

They were arresting known drug dealers in those areas that the drug flooded the most. Questioning them about, where they got them from?

Did they have any crooked relatives in the police department? They even questioned police officers that were over the evidence room. Making them take lie detector tests. Going into bank accounts to see which officers had unexplainable sums of money in their accounts. And the officer driving the U-haul, It was chaos in the city as well as inside the precinct all because of this crooked ass mother fucker.

He arrived at the precinct with a note attached to his desk, the Captain wanted to see him.

"Detective, You know the boys from Internal Affairs!" he nodded to the two white men that were sitting in his office. When they both turned to greet him, he watched his Captain side eye them. His Captain was Hispanic; he knew that black and brown was in this secret tug of war of color with whites.

"Gentlemen, Det. Duncan said greeting them and shaking their hands. What in the hell could they possibly want with him?

"These Gentlemen would like to ask you some questions in regards to the shipment that you were a part of seizing back in 2011. They are also requiring you being hooked up to a lie detector after the questioning."

"Are you also questioning my partner at the time, a Det. Thomas Branson?"

"Well, we have spoken with Thomas about the issue and we asked him for his cooperation in this matter. Since he is no longer a police officer, we can't insist he take a lie detector test, unless he is under arrest."

"Excuse me, my detective and I would like to get this straight, that you are insisting that he takes a lie detector test and you are not "insisting", that a disgruntled ex-cop, that was known for his misconduct, bullying, scrupulous activities and arrest records, a man that has no respect and have shown no respect for his "Ethnic" superiors nor his ethnic fellow officers. This man was questionable with even having an African American, Hispanic American and any other Non-white Officers back in the line of duty. And here we have a model Officer, that even has the recognition for his ethics from former Mayor Scott King and you want to take him through a lie detector test as if he would be the ideal suspect in this situation. You moth-"

"Captain, I have no problem with taking a lie detector test. Let's get this over with."

Det. Duncan past the lie detector test, of course. He left out of the precinct livid. He pulls out his cell ready to make a call but thought better of it; he would just go see him, himself.

"How is she doing? He said walking into the Hospital room.

"She is going to be fine. The Doctor said she had a small amount in her system. But I'm thankful you found her when you did and giving her that shot saved her life. We owe you, thank you for saving her life." Nigel got up to shake his hand.

"Not a problem that's my job. If you owe me one then tell me the real reasons you are going after Det. Branson?"

Nigel gave him the basics; he left out everything except for the kidnapping and the heist. "Here is his address. Just make sure you leave us a trail that leads us to get that racist mother fucker. You don't have to leave him. And I'm not going to say a mother fucking thing. The safety of any one's child most definitely comes first before this fucking job." He was mad that he had to go through that shit at the precinct and he was going to take a page from Thomas's book and be a crooked nigga too.

Duncan left with his mind on a whirlwind.

This prick had the audacity to kidnap these people's children. Then he caused a wave of genocide. Killing off what seems to be a total reaching the hundreds of his people. He didn't care if they were drug users, but they could also just curious just like Truth. And with the kidnapping of her child, he could understand why she wanted to escape reality.

Nigel was praying, "I fucked up again, he heard a faint voice say. He looked up with a smile on his face.

"What do you mean?", he got up and closed the door. He walked right back to her side, grabbing her hand.

"I fucked up with Teesha because I was letting my emotions get the best of me and I ended up not getting the information we needed for Semaj. Due to everything getting to me I stole some cocaine from my best friend, something that would have brought our baby girl home and I snorted it during yet another important time that could have brought our children home. Am I such a fucked up mother that I'm self-sabotaging getting our children? Am I really that fucked up inside?" Truth was in tears.

Nigel looked down and the floor, he needed to address his wife with kid gloves. Her doctor told him that anything can send her over the edge, that was why he stayed in the streets, he was trying to get back in touch with the streets. So, he could find the children. He didn't want her to reach that edge so he went hard and in that process, he realized he hasn't been there to help her cope. A tear escaped and they wouldn't stop cascading down. "Naw, you are nowhere near a fucked up mother. I was raised by a fucked up mother. Everybody handles shit differently and I should have been there for you. As your husband, as your friend and as your partner, I should have been there to help you cope. I apologize for that! As far as, Teesha that needed to be done. He patted her on the hand, I found some of the money in her house. And I have spoken with Det. Duncan."

Tisha felt relieved, as Nigel updated her on what was going on. "He gave me the address of Det. Branson."

"Why in the hell are you still here?" she said painfully trying to sit up.

"All in due time, I can't bring our baby girl home if mommy isn't okay."

"Believe mommy is okay now, she said looking down at the badges across her ribs, Now go get our kids."

She was still in pain, they found out in the midst of her trying to stand and get to the door, she fell on the coffee table hit her head and fractured her ribs.

They came in and gave her more medicine. That is when Nigel decided he needed to go handle the detective.

Nigel called Genesis and told her what happened, she rushed over to the hospital. He then told her, what the cop said, what he told him and how much he told him. That way if he came back through she would know what to say. And if the cops come around don't say anything about the Det. Duncan, just to tell them she was at a party, she asked for a cigarette she didn't smoke it until she got home and that is when she got sick, her husband came home to find her passed out and brought her here.

Nigel was going to suit up for war, "Yes, tonight would be the night he will get his Baby Girl back." He could feel it in his soul. He was too ecstatic but not too much of in a good mood he couldn't kill. He hated to leave his wife but he left her a note, "Going to get our Baby Girl! I love you, NO MATTER WHAT!"

Chapter 16

Nigel had left his wife's side in an angry frenzy lead by the information Det. Duncan had. He knew who was behind the kidnapping and his insides were beating him up for not figuring it out who the white cop was that everyone said set everything up.

He hit the steering wheel so hard he twisted his wrist springing it in the process of his rage. Attention by Kevin Gates fed his pain through his car speakers. It fed his anger it announced his arrival and it stayed on repeat. He did not feel the pain shooting through his hand. He only felt the pain of his failure to find out who kidnap the children sooner.

He arrived at Det. Branson address, the neighborhood was quietly covered in darkness. Attention you are in the presence of a Gangsta chanted inside his head like his anthem. It set the scene but he hoped that the deadly screams of the Detective did not awaken the nosey neighbors of this predominantly white neighborhood. He hoped his cries of pain went in sync with the lyrics of his arrival. He got out the car with a knife, bat, and gun hidden in his coat, studying his surroundings.

No one knew he was death. No one would be aware of his intentions. No one would hear him announcing his arrival in his head, Attention you are in the presence of a Gangsta. He would not break in, death would knock on this mother fucker's door and he would know his name is Nigel King.

And he would know that he was death.

He would know why death came a knocking.

He knocked and turned his back towards the door, again checking to see if the late night peepers were lurking in their slumber, instead of in their windows. Hoping no one was noticing the Black Gangsta of death knocking to do his bidding. He would hate to have to go kill them, he was not into collateral damage but he will collect on their lives if need be.

No answer.

He pressed the doorbell.

Still no answer.

He tried the doorknob

It was unlocked.

He opened the door with a gun in hand, lurking in the dark listening to the sounds of the house, waiting to see proof of life, waiting to end life. He got a glimpse of a glowing light towards the back of the house.

He cautiously stepped into the living room to get a better view. This was a ranch style house, with no basement so he only had to worry about the danger that might be in front of him. He didn't know whether or not the Det.'s Beloved was dwelling at Hade's gate awaiting for her death also to arrive. He can give a fuck about killing a woman who was involved in endangering his family. They should find peace in dying together.

He slowly arrived at a closed door, opening it gently and nudging it all the way with his gun. He saw twin beds, it was evident it was one bed for a girl and one bed for a boy. The bedding of blue and yellow covered the beds individually.

The room was filled with toys he closed the bedroom door and searched around for the familiarity of the kids. He spotted a hoodie with King on it, that he knew belonged to his nephew.

Nigel picked the clothing up to get a closer look, no signs of blood. On the yellow bed folded up was a pink shirt he knew was his daughters. He smelled it to confirm, he inhaled her scent, the lingering faint smell of the washing detergent that his wife used. He checked for blood.

There was none. He heard stumbling outside of the door, he pulled the bat out of his trench coat and moved closer to the door. Was that the sound of his daughter, his nephew or the two mother fuckers that was soon to be dead? He heard cursing as someone was struggling to get up, only to slip and fall again. Once he heard the person move past the door he slightly open it to peer out.

There he was, pasty, bloated and white, drunkenly talking to himself, Det. Thomas Branson was walking around in his boxers with a bottle of Scotch in his hand. He looked to be distressed over something. He appeared to be in turmoil, instead of attacking, he waited.

Det. Thomas Branson

Thomas stumbled around, guzzling his bottle of scotch devastated over his Beloved disappearing. He loved her, sure he still despise niggers but he loved her. He hated their darker skin rather it was just a hint of melanin in it or not, but he loved her skin. He had kissed her skin, took her dark nipples into his mouth to suckle upon its sweetness.

He grabbed his cock as the visions of her and her curly silky hair running through his fingers. He hated their curly, wavy, kinky greased scalps. but, he adored hers especially when she got out of the shower freshly shampooed and conditioned. He marveled at the beauty of her curls. He loved it even when she straightened it with what she called flat irons. He hated the scent of niggers. But, the cocoa butter and coconut oil she moisturized her skin with still filled the sheets with her fragrance.

He staggered into the bedroom, taking another gulp and flopping face first into the sheets on the bed that still held her scent. He crawled to her side of the bed, grabbing her pillow into his arms, holding it tightly, sobbing like a drunken wounded creature.

He tried to hide his hatred for her people. His mind went over everything he said. He did not use the N-word around her. Did somehow she sense that he belittled their existence on this earth? Those times that he thought she was sleeping did she hear him in his drunken stupors, plotting his want to kill off the Black race. Did she figure out his plan to spread out a deadly tainted drug throughout the black communities? He thought he was careful not to reveal his truth.

He tried to jump out of bed, to go to the office. The humming of the computer screen, the light from the monitors reminded him that he left up a map lining out the black and Latino communities that he wanted to distribute the drugs in, once he heard the police scanners and news reports. He made sure he cross-referenced it with his map to make sure they hit their targets. It was only then he would give them their children back.

Thomas was now drunk with madness looking at the map, he had killed damn near a hundred niggers and wetbacks in 72 hours. And they were still unsure of the body count because those fucking monkeys and run for the border mother fuckers were still coming in by the dozens of the tainted cocaine in their systems. And no one would ever think to pen him the genocidal mastermind behind it all, He laughed out loud, hysterically at the thought of it all.

He took another gulp of his bottle and laughed and started ranting out loud, "The Lake County Police department, Internal affairs, The DEA and The FBI called him in for his help. They needed to know who the Big drug dealers in the areas that the tainted drugs were sold in. They knew who they were but they haven't studied them over the years like I have. Ha, I gladly gave them the names of those men and women. They needed me," he laughed again and pointed to himself, "Me!"

The list was those of niggers and spics that he couldn't get convicted that he had arrested for drug trafficking. "Those street niggers knew I didn't go by the book. That, I was never there to serve and protect their asses. Hun, yes I took their dope, money, guns, and jewelry when I pulled them over or went to their house for a bust. Me and a lot of others that were secretly in the Brotherhood." He started naming names of those who were doing dirt against Blacks and Hispanics.

"I had beaten some and shot a lot of niggers that ran from me or I let them get away in hopes they would lead me to their Bosses or pay me not to send them to jail. But, who cares, he said laughing, they were niggers selling dope to other pathetic junky niggers and spics. They were killing their own kind anyway. Black on Black crime, Brown on Brown crime, Black on Brown crime. Who cared about the superior white man cleaning the streets of niggers? I'm a good old boy, I just didn't wear a white sheet over my head, I wore a badge on my chest.

Then the IA, asked," me if I could help them by identifying any rogue cops, cops who would have the knowledge of when and where the secret location of the drug disposal plan was located?" He stopped ranting to take another swig of alcohol. The shit was still swimming in his head. He didn't know what they were talking about. He came in thinking he was going to have to look at footage of someone breaking into the Evidence room.

He had returned home seething, those mother fuckers did not do the heist as planned. This made it hard for him to get back at the Police Department for making him go into early retirement, for making a mockery of him for getting his nose broken by a 14-year-old that little black bitch, for dismissing his word over those criminal ass monkeys. Scared that Farrakhan, Al Sharpton or some fucking nigger leader was going to come down on the force. What happened to the camaraderie of the badge? We protect our own, went out the fucking window. I had shot and killed a lot of nigger criminals and got away with it, since when did Black Lives Matter.

He had come home wanting his Beloved to calm him, comfort him and even see her play with those kids. He wanted her to get angry with him, but she was gone and the kids were gone. His emotions went to one high down to another.

He started talking to himself again out loud, he staggered down the hall, to turn on the shower. His victory was bittersweet because he didn't have his Beloved to share this moment with. Where did she go? Why did she leave with them? Why did she leave him? He had to find her. "Kill me, God.!" He proclaimed

Chapter 17

Sabrina awoke screaming hysterically she did not recall coming here, she did not even recall making herself a bath or getting in it, Why was it a pinkish color as if blood was, she looked down at her arms, legs and torso there were cuts all over her, creating the pinkish, reddish hue that was in the water.

Survival kicked in as she tried to remove herself out of the water, she couldn't her arms and legs were chained to the bottom of the tub,

"Hellllllppp! She said crying, feeling the sting of the multitude of cuts on her body.

"Heeeeellllp me! She screamed again.

"Nobody can hear you but the left for DEAD!" Genesis said smoking a Cuban cigar. Sabrina hated those things with a passion, she said it reminded her of her abusive father. Conjured up memories she spent her adulthood trying to forget.

Sabrina didn't like the look on her lover's or should she say ex-lover's face. Candles were lit around the room giving off an eerie vibe and look to the bathroom. Genesis was sitting on the toilet across the room like she was on a throne. And she was the High Priest of Death! She had been watching Sabrina for 20 minutes waiting for her to gain consciousness.

"Why?"

"I did what I did because you didn't love me anymore. I did it because you always put them before me, especially Sorrow. I wanted to be the most important person in your life, so I decided to take Det. Branson up on his offer. But, when I saw what they did to you, I knew shit went too far."

"You want to hit this, she offered her the blunt.

"Yes, Sabrina did not know what offering her the blunt meant. Did this mean she was forgiven? What the hell did this shit mean?

Genesis carried her closed bucket with her, she sat on the floor next to Sabrina's head and set the bucket next to her. She brought the blunt to Sabrina's mouth several times so she could hit it. She then threw it in her water and grabbed another one out of her pocket lit it and started smoking.

She smiled up at Sabrina and laughed, "You so full of shit!, I wouldn't fucking dare smoke after a grimy bitch like you. You have so much larceny in your heart, you don't know when the fuck somebody would actually love yo ass." She opened the bucket and carefully threw a leech in the water. Immediately the creature flocked to Sabrina's bleeding flesh ready to partake, ready to devour.

Sabrina didn't think it felt so bad, there was no pain from what she through in the water, "Do you know where the kids are?"

"No, I honestly don't!" Genesis believed her

"You know I'm not with this whole torturing shit like Sorrow, especially if your ass don't have any information that I need. From the beginning, I knew you wasn't about the right, but I fell in love anyway. Ready to help you become a better you, you did not succeed in that. How the fuck do you plan a kidnapping of the children, that you know that I love to death. What was your logic behind this shit? I know exactly what you wanted bitch. You didn't want me, you did not do this fucked up shit to better our relationship. How in the fuck could you believe that it would? You did this shit because you're money hungry. You wanted that money. You could have given two shits about me or my family. Tell the truth and shame the devil. Well, you don't need too. it was and it will always be about the money, no matter who you fuck over. You fucked your son over he had a happy home with me. I took your ass in when you were pregnant with him after you cheated on me and left and gotten pregnant by that nigga. I watched your son be born, that nigga was nowhere to found. I took care of him. I still loved you but I didn't trust you. But, I would have never thought that I would have to watch my back around your ass. I would have never thought that you would use the nigga, I had saved you from to kill me. "

Sabrina started crying because she knew she was right. She knew her life was over but she also knew that Genesis would make sure her son was okay. Genesis rose up from her sitting position and just poured all the leeches inside of her bath water.

They latched on, she was trapped with no possibilities of removing them from sucking what was left of blood in her. The sucking was weird feeling but not painful. She still screamed, fighting with her body to remove them, she twisted her body so hard she threw some of the water out of the tub, wetting the flames of some candles to extinguish.

Genesis walked out on her, leaving her to die alone. Something else Sabrina had expressed to her, she had a fear of dying alone. She didn't know how long it would take for the leeches to help bleed her out but she would come check on her in about an hour.

By then she should be dead.

Genesis got a text and left hurriedly. She tried calling Sorrow but, she was not answering the phone.

Sorrow

Nobody has heard anything from the kidnappers since the outbreak. Sorrow was going crazy she did everything they had wanted. She was in tears when she finally got her text. "453."

Nigel

Nigel was glad he waited to attack him. He was videotaping every word of his drunken rant of bragging, he tried to demolish a city of people, two races of people. He watched as Thomas plopped his fat pale ass down on a chair sitting in front of the computer after he came back from the bathroom. Nigel heard the shower running. Nigel decided to take a page from his sister's book, he hid in the darkness and found his song *Spell On You by Bingo on The Track ft. Suave Bos,* he rolled his head around to loosen his neck, he rolled his shoulders back and cracked his knuckles. Nigel gripped his bat and he slowly walked towards the detective.

The room was spinning for Thomas, he couldn't focus properly, but he saw the dark figure coming towards him in what seemed like slow motion. He smiled, he laughed as he swung his chair around to fully face what was coming towards him. "You're too late nigger, I don't know where the fuck your porch monkeys are?" he laughed hysterically and took a swig of his bottle but there was no liquid. He had finished it off. It was the end.

Nigel swung the bat at his head so hard his head snapped to the side he raised the bat again and again.

Hitting him again and again.

Blood splattered and decorated the walls with each connection of the bat. Nigel's mind was lost in an oblivion of hate, his animosity was plentiful it couldn't be quenched with the blood he was shedding. Something in him egging him on, this mother fucker was around your daughter and nephew. His filthy pasty hands touched them, his lips curled up and he snarled as he repeatedly beat his head in with the bat.

He was not appeased with the chunks of brain matter falling from the detective's head, still with pieces of it clinging to his bat, he connected with his head again and again the cracking sound of his skull released him from his fury.

He set the bat down and with his gloves still on he hooked his cell into the man's laptop and sent it to all his email contacts, which were mostly his ex-brothers in blue. Nigel took his fingers and dipped the tips of them into the puddles of blood, on the wall he had written POWER TO THE PEOPLE. He grabbed the chair and threw Thomas onto the floor, he erased everything dealing with the kidnapping.

The footage, the electronic hacks into their phones, he turned off and erased the cameras he had connected to their homes also. The phone he was using to contact them were sitting next to the laptop, he erased all the names involved except for Teesha's contact and the times he had called her. He deleted the text messages though. It had vital information linked to him and his family. He then searches for his phone provider, found that he kept his account opened and erased those messages also.

He needed to destroy the laptop so when he realized that the shower was still running he plugged the tub up and let it fill up. He went grabbed the laptop and all his electronics and dumped them all in the tub. He searched for bleach anything he could find to add to the damage of the electronics. He found acid, ammonia and bleach.

Nigel didn't question why his ass had acid, but he grabbed it all and poured it on the laptops. He saved the acid, he was careful not to waste any on him, he had to hurry because the fumes were getting to him, he then poured the acid onto Det. Thomas Branson's body. The acid ate away at his flesh, had he still been alive that would have been tremendous torture for him.

Before Nigel could think of any more damage to fulfill his deadly wrath, he got a text from

Sorrow he hurriedly eased his way back out the house. He was sure the kids were no longer in his home. So, who in the fuck was Beloved and where did she take the kids?

Chapter 18

Sorrow stood dumbfounded at the sight of her childhood home, memories and nightmarish scenes plagued her mind. A once thriving and lively street was now a grotesque shell of what it once was, family houses were now abandoned and left to squatters. Debris decorated the dying lawns, boarded up windows, houses were being raped of its guts, just like the homeowners were raped for their safety and forced to find their protection elsewhere.

The street was avoided of all light, and so was her heart. The scenery could have been right out of a slasher classic. Freddy could be standing there with his finger of knives or Jason could be standing in front of 453 with a machete. Sorrow cocked her gun and patted her waist to secure the other one, neither one of them mother fuckers could fuck with Queen Black Panther right now.

She checked her surroundings no sign of Malakai, Nigel or Genesis. If the Apocalypse was happening right now that couldn't even stop her from going inside to see if her son and niece were also caged in her childhood home.

Sorrow crept in the door with her gun drawn, every memory about this house tortured her mind as she tried to stay focused on the sounds in the house.

Flashes of every beaten, every harsh word, and every emotional anguish Chenille had bestowed upon her built up her anger towards whoever, whoever had the audacity to make her step foot in this godforsaken place again.

If the kids were in here how dare this person bring them to this house of hatred. It wasn't all hatred but it was more hatred than love dwelling behind these walls.

Before she went upstairs she stopped in her tracks as she listened to the humming coming from downstairs out of the basement. A lullaby was being hummed through the vents that voice was not familiar to her yet it made her chest ache with fear for the children.

She follows the singing downstairs, a lump was in her throat as she walked closer and closer to the figure holding 2 toddlers in their arms.

Sorrow could smell her child, she could hear her child's soft voice utter the word, Grandma. Tears swell up in Sorrow's eyes making her vision blurry but not too blurry that she could not recognize her son skin tone, not too blurry that she could not see her son's curly crown. This moment was bittersweet because how could she predict the moves of the person holding them.

She grips her gun steadily moves her body in front of the rocking chair, holding her child was a ghost a nightmarish monster that Sorrow never ever wanted her son or niece to meet. Until this very moment, she thought she had an achieved that goal in life.

"Hello, it's nice that you let me spend time with my grandchildren," she said with a sinister grin. Sorrow eyes would grow darker in a moment like this but they grew almost of pale light grey something was stirred up in sorrow that no one in this world could conjure up but Chenille King.

"You can put your gun down I would hate for you to accidentally shoot one of these beautiful children. Beside by the time you pull the trigger. I'm going to make these babies dope fiends just like their grandmother. Just like your black ass should've been! I spent years trying to destroy your life. But I'm the one that ended up on drugs. No matter how bad I tried to damage your image amongst my boys and my husband you always seemed to be the one they came to protect. Have a seat right there." Chenille told her as she held both of the needles towards the kid's' legs.

" You evil demonic bitch. If you wanted me you should have come after me. Not my fucking child! Not my fucking niece." Sorrow never put her gun down or moved it away from Chenille's head.

Chenille never noticed that Sorrow never put her gun down she went into her head and her own evil daydream. They both had tried to kill her, her son and her daughter. She could understand Sorrow but Nigel her jealous mind could not understand why Nigel would leave her for dead.

Chenille continues to talk, "I stayed in that closet for days until Kennedy nosey ass came around snooping for shit to sell. I know what your brother was hoping your brother was hoping I would die on my own. I would rot in that closet, seeing that he wasn't dead filled me with so much will. You couldn't imagine the strength that hate and revenge could give you, the again maybe you can. 7 long years, I waited and I planned this moment. Your enemies fell right into my lap. They wanted the same thing I wanted. They wanted to see you fail they wanted to see you fall right in front of everyone who adores you. To prove once and for all that Black Pantha was just some stupid unloved Black Bitch from the ghetto. Nobody special."

"I had that old washed up, little dick pale mother fucker thinking he was in control of this whole operation. Merely a pawn at best. He was the face of it all, he was taking the most risks. It's unfortunate, that all those lives were taken because of his racist ass. but nevertheless I had to keep on with my plan."

"Ha, he kept going on and on about the little black bitch who broke his nose and the King brothers. Especially, Nigel whom he said he knew he took the fall for you in that Duke case. He was given a lesser sentence because he was stopping Duke from killing you. And Malakai he hated him too out on a technicality because of Teesha. The case was reopened because her confession was recorded and her description of the man who murdered her cousins that night fit the description of your brother. But of course, they couldn't prove that Nigel did it. Cases after cases were getting thrown out because of his racist misconduct after that. He felt you all were his downfall in his law enforcement career. I was proud of the little black bitch that broke his nose. He blamed everything on you and my beloved boys. And here he was in love with the very person who gave birth to you all. Haha, the old bitch still got it." She laughed.

"You do know that Det. Branson is the same racist cop that use to kill black men around the neighborhood it didn't matter to him if they were criminals or not? And he is the reason behind over a hundred deaths in Gary from the last week."

"I'm aware of the hatred he had for Blacks and Hispanics. Please, Am I supposed to shed a tear over some crack heads losing their lives. Nobody gave a fuck about me, not even my own children when I was a crackhead. So why should I give them any type of sympathy? It seems to me like he did the black community a favor. Besides they were casualties of war. Minor lives for my major moves." Chenille shrugged it off as if the poisoning of 100 something black people were a mere hangnail, she could overlook.

"You are still a fucking coward, Chenille," she told her while shaking her head. Sorrow kept her eyes on those needles and Chenille, contemplating her next move. Her son and niece were fast to sleep. She didn't like them being comfortable in her mother's arms. She wanted to throw up as she watched her rock them back and forth, the idea of her hands even touching them sent her aching heart into a frenzy.

Chenille kept going as if Sorrow had not uttered a word. While she watched Chenille she heard the slight noise above her head. Chenille with her eyes closed kept talking, "You know why I hated you. I hated you because they loved you. Every man in my life loved my mistake but didn't love me. Your father loved you even in my womb. That day in the delivery room, I had to tell James about Hunter. He called your father and I was devastated at how fast he brought his ass up there. He took one look at your black ass and signed those papers. His mother and he told me he could have never given a woman like me his last name. But, he makes sure his daughter had the world. I canceled that shit, especially when I found out his loving wife was just so in love with you. The bitch was ready to accept her husband's bastard ass child. I called the authorities on his kingpin ass and he had no choice but to hide his black ass back in Haiti. I'm not going to even get on the call the High and mighty Evelyn had given me. That's why I had you kill that bitch and destroy your own birth right."

"Let me not get on Sabrina, Bobbie, Teesha, and Alexus all had malice in their hearts for you or someone in your crew. Boy, it is a lot of lurking hating people in this world. At least you can give me credit for not being a fake bitch."

Nigel

Nigel entered the house through the broken back door, a gust of wind blew the rain through the windowless frames of what once was the kitchen window. Nigel took off his shoes in the filth and debris. He was careful where he steps as not to make a sound or to step on anything that could damage his feet. The text Sorrow sent just stated, *453 911 basement*, that was all he needed to know and he knew exactly where she was. He wondered who in the hell could have led her back to that hell hole?

As he managed to slowly go down the stairs undetected, he heard her voice and his hate for her had bubbled up inside of him and when he saw her from the back holding their children, despising his own mother had resurfaced at a level within enemy territory. As he reached the end of the stairs his gun was pointed at her head and so was Sorrow's. Chenille did not feel, nor hear him coming up behind her, her venting off her hatred for Sorrow took her to a place of tunnel vision.

Chenille's arms were relaxed as she spilled out her truth, she no longer held the needles directly on the children's flesh, her thumb no longer threaten to push down on the syringe. He couldn't see why Sorrow wouldn't just put one in her. "Mommy, Hunter said finally awake leaping out of Chenille's arms that was Nigel's cue, she tried to quickly snatch him back but Sorrow was too quick she grabbed him and as Chenille jumped forward she snatched Hunter towards her and snatched Semaj up at the same time.

Nigel grabbed the barrel of his gun and whacked it against Chenille's temple, she lost her balance, falling head first on the concrete floor. She was out cold.

Nigel grabbed his daughter, Semaj realized who was holding her and her little arms wrapped around his neck so tight, "My Daddy! She cried, "You found us! You found us! Daddy you and Auntie Sorrow are bad at hiding seek."

Nigel let tears fall from his eyes as he gave his baby girl kisses all over her face. He put her down, "Daddy pick me up, pick me up. I don't want you to not find me again." She whined

"Baby, never again, never again will Daddy not find you. Are you hurt? He said looking her over. Did they hurt you?" he said in a panic.

"Don't cry daddy, Grandma not hurt us. See daddy, she said touching her hair, Grandma said I pretty with my beads. She gave me beads so I can make noise." She said shaking her hair so the beads could swing and make noise.

"Yeah, Baby Girl, you are beautiful," he said forcing a smile on his face. He looked at his daughter and noticed her hair was French braided with colorful beads. She had on a new outfit and shoes as well. She was clean, she looked like her normal happy self. He looked over at his sister as she clung to her son, holding him tightly, rocking him back and forward in her arms, crying uncontrollably.

He had never seen his sister this vulnerable since she was a child enduring the abuse of their mother. He pulled out his phone and texted MG, "Where are you? 453 Jackson basement ASAP." He took a picture of Sorrow and his nephew and sent it to Malakai.

Malakai

"Det. Thomas Branson, that fat white mother fucker is behind this shit." Nigel screamed into the phone. Malakai was almost at the house in Illinois. If Sorrow wouldn't come back to Miller, he would come to her.

"Why didn't we think of his ass? That shit makes perfect sense, that mother fucker couldn't even arrest us back in the day. He always made his ass mad because he never could catch us dirty. That's the same mother fucker nose Sorrow broke when that shit happend with you and Big King back in the day. She humiliated that racist mother fucker in front of his brothers in blue. He was the cop that questioned Teesha about that

Chicago, shit. Why in the fuck didn't we think of his ass?" Malakai said pissed

"And he was the arresting officer in the Duke, Jason, and Co- Co case but you see how that shit went for him," Nigel added

"You know where he's at! Do you know if he got the kids?"

"On my way there now. I will let you know if the kids are at the address that Det. Duncan gave me. That pig has to go!" he said hanging up.

Malakai pulled into his garage, he found a big black mother fucker guarding his home. He had pulled out his gun and jumped out the car. The man had his gun drawn also, as they recognized each other they lowered their weapons.

What the fuck did Sorrow have going on at his fucking house? He wondered.

He entered his home not knowing what he would find or who he will find, his home was heavily guarded. He had to blink twice when she stepped out of the guest bedroom to greet him. He didn't know rather he should hug her and drop to his knees and pray.

Before he could ask questions, he received a picture message, he waited for it to load. He teared up and relief washed over him and he did drop to his knees and thank God, praised God and worshipped Him! He didn't care about the guards or who was standing in front of him.

Panic raised in the woman for she thought he was sent bad news, she grabbed his phone out of his hand and started giving thanks. Malakai rose from his knees and went right back out the house, he speeded to Gary, Indiana headed for 453!

Nigel

Then he sent a picture to Truth of Semaj, with a message, "I got our Baby girl! I got her and she is cool. We are "complete again, baby!"

Truth

Truth screamed out in joy and wept into her pillow filled with relief and pain. She needed to hold her baby girl. She texted him, "Bring her straight to me."

Sorrow

"Mommy! Mommy! You missed the hell out of me. Grandma said you will. But, you taking the air out of me."

Sorrow laughed through her tears as she let up on him just a little, she started placing kisses on his face. "I forgot that you are mommy's big boy. I just missed you so much." Sorrow sat back down in the chair and put him down. And looked at him eye to eye, his beautiful gray eyes were still filled with innocence. She placed his hands on hers, "Did anybody hurt you?"

He shook his head no, "Why are you cry?" he asked trying to wipe her tears.

"Because mommy missed the hell out of you!"

"Well, how come you not find me fast? I told Grandma you always win, but you took forever. So, I win this time. Right Mommy?"

Sorrow looked down at Chenille still unconscious, "You told Gran- she couldn't even say it. She would be damned if she would acknowledge this bitch as his Grandmother when she didn't even deserve the title of mother. "You told her right! Mommy always wins except against you. King!"

"And sometimes Daddy too, Mom." He stated matter of fact

"Yeah and sometimes Daddy! But, most of the time I win against him too," she said with a chuckle

Hunter started looking around, "Hey, Uncky King!

Nigel walked over to him and gave him a big hug, "Hey, Big guy!" Sorrow placed a kiss on Semaj's forehead and gave her a tight hug, her eyes teared up again as she hugged her niece.

"Hey, Te Te, You not so good at hide seek, like daddy, she said shaking her head.

Sorrow laughed, "Yeah, I guess not!"

"Umm, Mom, Hunter said patting her on her arm trying to get her attention, "You gonna wake up Grandma and tell her you and Uncky won. Slow. She said if you did she was going to give you a prize."

"Oh, believe me, she knows." She side eyeing Chenille with a dark look on her face, she then caught herself and smiled at her son. "And your cousin and you are the prizes."

Nigel's phone indicated he had a text to inform him Malakai was on his way in, a couple of seconds later Malakai ran down the stairs with his gun in his hand. Ready. Ready to kill anything and anyone, he stopped in his tracts and tucked his gun in the back of his pants, as he heard the laughter of the children.

His heart cried joyously on the inside when he saw his little man talking to his mom and his niece standing next to him. He wanted to drop to his knees and cry. He silently thanked God. His son didn't notice he entered the room but he noticed everything about him in a split second.

Hunter hair was freshly braided and lined up, he had on new clothes and shoes, he didn't look to have a bruise or scratch on him. That made him look Semaj up and down, and she too looked as if she was cared for instead of kidnapped. They both were smiling and seem unbothered by the situation.

You never hear of positive outcomes of kidnappings. You hear of molestation, sexual abuse, physical abuse, mental abuse, and death. A child coming home after a month or so with new clothes, fresh do with no care in the world was unheard of, they weren't even crying, there were no traces of them being frightened.

Malakai was grateful but still wondered who would have kidnapped children and taken care of them. Don't get him wrong he was still ready to murder them, he just wanted to know why and who. He walked further down and into the basement, he saw a figure on the floor, it was a woman. He walked over to the body and lifted her head up, he was puzzled, he was confused.

He stood over her body in a trance, he would have never thought she would be the one even if she wasn't supposed to be dead. He would have never thought Chenille King would have pulled something like this off. But the capabilities of evil could not be underestimated.

Nigel acknowledges Malakai with a head nod and tapped Hunter on his shoulders. Hunter ran into his arms, "Daddy! Daddy! Mom was slow but she always wins right. But you were slower to find me."

He held him tight and places his lips on the top of his head he stood there with him in his arms not quite squeezing him but secured his body with his arms.

Semaj came in for a hug too, "Uncle Poochie, I was found slow too in the hide seek game. Give me hugs and kisses." She demanded.

Malakai laughed, as he looked at his wife. She was drained but he could see the joy and liberation on her face. He could also see the darkness brewing, the hate steaming and rising to the top. She was not satisfied with just the return of her child or her niece. No, the look on her face told a tale of vengeance. Now, that he knew who was behind it, he knew this was a personal attack on his wife.

Genesis came running down the stairs Truth had contacted her from her hospital bed and informed her that the children were found and where they were found. She also was curious as to who would bring the children to Sorrow's childhood home. Who was evil enough to stir up that kind of a pain in her friend?

When the children saw Genesis they ran to her and she embraced them with tears in her eyes.

Auntie G, we saw the bad men hurt you. I was scared you dead," Semaj confessed

During this whole ordeal that was the most frightening part for the children being snatched up by unknown people and seeing Genesis beat up. "You don't call me Auntie G for nothing, baby." She said downplaying the incident.

"Yeah, Maj that's why they call her Gangsta G," Hunter said patting Genesis on the shoulder.

"Hey, you guys go with Auntie G, she's going to take you to the car." Sorrow told them

"No more slow hide seek. Okay, mommie. Cause I don't want to miss the hell out of you!"

Sorrow walked over to her son, "No more slow hide seek, ever again. And King don't say hell again, it's a grownup word." She said kissing her son.

She then whispered in his ear, "Mommy has to go out town to work for a couple of days. I need you to be good and take care of Daddy."

He whispered back in her ear, "Okay!"

Genesis finally saw the body on the floor, she looked up at them for answers. She mouthed, "Who the fuck is that?"

Nobody wanted to answer her, this was a complicated situation. They didn't want to say what they were feeling and they didn't want G to say something alarming to the kids because she didn't know that in the children's head they thought they were visiting with their Grandmother playing a long ass game of hide and seek. It was a different game for the seekers.

"Mommy, are you going to tuck Grandma in her bed?"

Genesis looked at the body still lying on the floor and then she looked at Sorrow. Sorrow held her gaze and Genesis saw the familiar depths of fury in her eyes, "Oh, King, I'm going to tuck her in so tight she will see God." The venom in her voice was like acid dripping on flesh.

Genesis knew that was her cue to lead the kids out of the war's zone. When Sorrow heard the front door close she told them, "Lift this bitch up and tie her to that chair." Sorrow instructed.

"Poochie, go get those liquid filled blue bullets from the black bag in my trunk and the blow torch. Please."

After he and Nigel finished tying her up to the chair, he did just that and came back holding the whole black bag. She smiled inside because her husband knew her so well. Who knows what other weapons she would want to use on Chenille?

Her brother and husband stood like soldiers standing next to her undying pain, her nemesis, the woman who gave birth to her but was never her mother, waiting and ready to dispose her of her nightmarish hell. Sorrow breathed deeply, closed her eyes, she had buried this woman with respect. Why?

Why she did it under false pretenses? She knew Nigel was lying but she wanted to let her mind pretend that Chenille's dying words were her cleansing. It was a way to move on from the abuse. She had buried her past in that moment of forgiveness.

Sorrow opened her eyes, she peered at Nigel without content but the knowing was evident. Nigel held her gaze, she knew he was only trying to help her heal. But, he couldn't help her now and neither could her husband. He nodded at Sorrow and left.

Malakai felt the her she once was, enter the room, and she was carrying a dangerously amount of wrath with her. He knew what she wanted him to do but he didn't want to leave her by herself. Not in this state, what would this do to her? She wanted to hear Chenille's hate for her, she wanted to know why there was so much hate towards her.

Malakai knelt before his wife and cupped her face, she placed her hand on his heart and kissed him deeply. He felt her love, he felt her forgiveness and he felt her understanding in that kiss. And he knew that what he did was understood and forgiven.

"I love you greater than I love myself." He told her

"I love you greater than I love myself," she repeated

He kissed her tear stained face and looked at her deeply in her eyes. "I need to do this alone." She said answering the question his eyes were asking.

"Okay, baby." He walked away leaving Sorrow alone with her mother.

Sorrow injected Chenille with a blizzard, it will take her a while to wake up. She went to her car and drove to the nearest Menards she bought boards, nails, hammer, toilet tissue, cleaning supplies, a small refrigerator a blow-up mattress, comforter, sheets and a toilet seat. She bought five packs of Newport, a box of vanilla wraps and a half of ounce of weed, water and even though her appetite was depleted she bought Lunchables. She laughed at herself old survival habits die hard.

As she got in the car a quote came to mind from one of her favorite books, "Bring war material with you from home, but forage on the enemy… use the conquered foe to augment one's own strength."

– Sun Tzu, the Art of War

This was most definitely the ending of a war that had started over three decades ago. It was a war that she thought she ended with closure and peace. But, her enemy resurfaced attacking her by capturing her most precious assets, using false friends and unknown enemies against her. Her enemy had infiltrated her camp with spies and visual weapons of control. Her camp was caught off guard which was a great strategy on Chenille's part. Then she alluded them by taking them through obstacles that would make them more enemies. Dangling the false hope of victory after each obstacle was conquered.

It was just like old times when she was out on the streets. Living in abandoned houses, curled up in the park, she needed to feel like it was old times. The past brought her to the place where the devil dwelled in her veins.

She arrived back at 453, she brought everything into the house and went downstairs to check on Chenille. She still had a pulse but she was still out of it. Sorrow sat and rolled up six blunts. She sat all her diabolical resurrections down on the table. She then went to the back and illegally turned on the electricity and the water, something she learned how to do when she was staying in houses that resembled the shambles of her current domicile.

She then boarded up the windows from the inside, she barricaded the doors, she fixed the back door so no one could enter it, she then barricaded the basement door inside the house, she left the basement door untouched for you could not get in from the outside. It was a steel door her step-father had installed it was only one way out.

Sorrow looked at her watch it had been five hours, it was time for the Devil to arise from her slumber. She sat her chair right in front of her and pulled on her blunt.

Chenille groggily had awakened in the same place, in the same chair, in front of the same person. But, she did not have the upper hand this time. Chenille through her head back and laughed.

"I know why I'm still alive. I know why you are still here." She told her amused.

"So, if you know let's quit with the bullshit and get on to the real bullshit." She smiled as she puffed her blunt she was just as amused.

"I knew you were going to be my enemy from the very moment you came out of my pussy wearing your father's skin and barring his eyes. I hated you to my core for not being my husband's daughter, for not having his skin and his eyes. I knew my fate was damaged and my marriage was doomed. You revealed my secrets. I was skilled in hiding my secrets, I took price in being careful with my infidelities, it was a rush to have a Handsome Black Drug Lord to take me to his bed time and time again. To shower me with gifts to surround me with an expensive taste that I didn't have the pleasure of having being a blue-collar worker's housewife. I despised you but I studied you, I saw the intelligence of your father in you and I knew that one day that intelligence would destroy me. So, I wanted to break your fucking spirit. So, I studied you, I glanced at the books you read and I learned a little. I never applied it until now.

"If you know the enemy and know yourself, you need not fear the result of a hundred battles. If you know yourself but not the enemy, for every victory gained you will also suffer a defeat. If you know neither the enemy nor yourself, you will succumb in every battle."

Sorrow raised her eyebrow and just nodded her head as she listened to Chenille King's final confessions. Sitting there listening as if she was a Catholic Priest, but there would be no forgiveness or instructions on how many Hail Mary's she should say to cleanse her of her sins. Sin is death. So, she must die.

"Maybe I was too doped up then, to really apply what I glanced at back then. I never spent a day sober after I had you. My hate grew as the men around me adored you, protected you and they cherished you like you were the Queen. So, I had to intoxicate myself damn near every hour on the hour, just to cope with the presence of you. You should be grateful it was because of weed, heroin, and crack that I didn't kill you or beat you to death. Often times I tried, I dreamed and daydreamed about your demise, probably as often as you dreamed of mine. Queen Black Pantha, the ghost of the drug world." Chenille laughed

"Are you surprised that I knew your little secret?"

Sorrow smirked, "Not at all. Kennedy always knew who I was, I personally gave him crack because I was tired of seeing you on your knees sucking dick for crack. A few times I wanted to put arsenic in there but I didn't because we both know Ken Ken is one greedy mother fucker."

Chenille felt a chill go down her back, she knew Sorrow was serious. She was now worried. It didn't seem that her decision to act like a Grandmother instead of a kidnapper worked in her favor. She wondered, should she have killed her grandchildren and sent them to her?

"When Thomas told me he thinks that Sorrow Hunter was this mysterious drug dealer that tortured and killed three people that he knows of, I was in disbelief, She looked around and down at her confinement to the chair, and continued, And now I'm starting to believe him."

Sorrow nodded again she did not admit to it nor committee to it. The only thought that was actually in her head was, "This bitch took my son. This bitch made me kill my Grandmother. This bitch almost killed my best friend. This Bitch was the reason Alexus was able to come after my husband. This Bitch is why my other best friend is lying in the hospital. This Bitch is part of the reason I was an accessory to genocide to my own city, my own people, I killed damn near 150 people. This Bitch is the reason why I have become the old me.

At some point Sorrow just saw Chenille's lips moving, she didn't hear a word. Flashes of the past entered her head. And she was that six-year-old girl again, in a pretty pink dress that she tried to impress her mother with, that ended her up being dragged through the backyard into a mud puddle. Forced to eat dirt.

She could still taste the sadness and the dirt that she was made to eat. She finally hears the rain, the thunder outside, the wind was howling. Revenge was chanting her name, revenge conjured up her dark past and turned her into that beautiful little black girl.

Rising up Sorrow untied the ropes, seconds went by as she just stared at her, hating her.

Remembering.

Sorrow punched Chenille in the face several times drawing blood from her nose. Disoriented, Chenille tried to block the hits, but couldn't

The blood loss and hits rendered her useless to her own defense. As, Sorrow grabbed her by her hair and dragged her to the basement door, the flashes of that pink dress day continued to play in her head. She unlocked and a swish of hard rain and wind tried to render her backward. Her anger refused to acknowledge it as she fought her way through the wind.

Chenille started kicking as the cold heavy rain hit her body her determination was not as dominate as Sorrow's. She felt her body hit the sidewalk, scraping up the back of her legs and back. It burned.

Sorrow found a nice mud puddle, she then took both hands, gripped her hair to flip her over. She continued to drag her face down into the mud puddle, she then jumped on top of her back in a straddling position and pushed her face into the mud. Suffocating her, filling her mouth and her nose full of mud, Chenille's screams only made it worse, as each scream brought more mud into her mouth.

Sorrow flipped her back over, she grabbed a wad of mud and force fed her, "You hungry you little yellow BITCH! If YOU'RE SO FUCKING HUNGRY EAT THIS!" she said reaching into her six-year-old mind recalling some of Chenille's word. Chenille gagged as she half swallowed and half spit out the mud.

Chenille emptied her mouth and laughed, "If this is what I made you experience I fucking Love it! I FUCKING LOVE IT YOU LITTLE BLACK BITCH!" she spat mud in Sorrow's face.

Sorrow started choking her, Chenille tried to claw at her hands, her hands were like a vice grip around her neck. Chenille felt herself losing consciousness. The rain poured down on them both as if God was trying to wash away their hate for each other before it was too late. Sorrow was deaf to God at this moment.

She rose up off of her and grabbed her by her hair again dragging her into the house. She was limp, Sorrow grabbed the syringe that she threatened the life of the children with, she replaced the liquid with another blizzard and she injected her ass with it, now she would really be out.

Sorrow decided not to tie her back to the chair, she used the rope to hang her by the beam in the ceiling. She tied her legs together and her hands behind her back. Sorrow gathered her belongings, washed away her sins, for now, ate and then laid down. She would rest up because tomorrow would be one hell of a day. For Chenille that is, she smiled up at her dangling from the ceiling. Sorrow went to sleep peacefully with her gun in her hand.

The next day, nobody had heard from Sorrow, she didn't answer her phone and finally, Malakai said fuck it and went over there. Everything was sealed up even the doors to enter the house. He couldn't panic because of his son, so he just left her a message. He called and told everyone what was going on, they too went over to see if they could get in the house.

No.

What was going on in there?

Sorrow woke up, Chenille was still out, she took a shower to refresh herself for today's activities. She drank some orange juice, ate an apple and banana.

She takes her blow torch and put fire to her poker, she then took the tip and started carving the letter B.

Instantly, Chenille wakes up screaming from the pain. Sorrow continues to carve Black Bitch in all Capital letters. "Wow, Mom we have matching tattoos, now." She said laughing as she showed her the picture of her back. Tears filled in Chenille's eyes, her breathing was becoming difficult and she fainted.

After about 30 minutes, "Hey, Mommy Dearest! She said quite cheerfully. She knew Chenille had to be hungry, thirsty, sore from hanging by her arms. She did not give one fuck. She continued eating her lunch in front of her, she saw the need in her eyes. But, she never asked for any of it, she just closed her eyes.

Maybe she should have just left the bitch alone. She could be long gone somewhere living her life without them even knowing she was still alive. But revenge got the better of her and she went for the kill. She forgot about karma, she forgot that karma was a bitch and this was hers coming back for its own revenge.

"Now, we need to see if you are a virgin. Wait, Sorrow said shaking her head cheerfully, you're my mom duh you can't be a virgin. But you can be a born-again virgin, let's see if you let that white man put his small little pasty pecker inside of you." Sorrow grabbed her trusty homemade bat and held it up to her.

Chenille's eyes widened as she saw the razor blades in the grooves of the bat. "Oh, you aren't used to this size. Hunh, don't worry mom I will be gentle. She slowly took the bat inside of her, it was like a desert. "Mom, come on you can't keep any man with that dry ass pussy. No wonder my dad said you weren't a keeper." Sorrow said shaking her head. Sorrow sprays the bat down, with lemon juice, cooking oil and alcohol a concoction she put together.

"What the fuck is that?' Chenille said her heart beating fast, hoping at some point and time Sorrow would give her whatever was in that needle she kept injecting into her. "Nooooo, she said as she felt her insides tear with each thrust and the burning of the spray made it worse.

Sorrow held it there, If I pull it out and it's bloody then you aren't a virgin. If I pull it out and it's clean, then my bad." She laughed

Where the fuck was this delightfully happy bitch coming from, she should still be enraged, cursing her out, she didn't understand her. Although Sorrow was fucking her up, she didn't want Sorrow to be happy.

Sorrow yanked it out fast, she heard the rips and tears of her mother's insides. "Oh, look at that. Not a virgin. Shame on you." Chenille threw her head back, she started vomiting, quickly Sorrow grabbed her head forward so she can vomit in the steel tub she had under her body.

Through the vomiting, she screamed as she saw a healthy amount of blood running down her legs. She felt light-headed and faint, she couldn't stay woke, she tried. Her eyes became blurry as she stared into the face of Sorrow. The evilness she had spawned was coming back to collect. She saw Sorrow's teeth as she came closer with a smile on her face and she then passed out.

Sorrow laughed, "I know a tough bitch like my momma can take some pain. I can take some pain, I guess you weren't raised by an evil, abusive bitch such as yourself." She said to her, she then grabbed a spray bottle of peroxide and a power washer, letting water spray her clean. The tainted water flowed into the drain. After she was cleansed Sorrow sprayed her with peroxide. It probably wasn't the best idea but then again she wasn't here to make the bitch comfortable.

Sorrow injected her with a blizzard and pulled her down off of the beam and laid her down. It was too early, she turned her phone back on and as soon as she did call after call came in and text after text. She knew what they wanted but there was no room for love right now. So, she quickly turned it back off.

Sorrow put Chenille's clothes in a tube full of gasoline she let it soak for two hours. She pulled everything she needed by the door. She taped Chenille's eyes closed placed her on the cushion. It was about 1 am in the morning, darkness had put two coats on the night sky and shielded the moon for what it was about to see. She left Chenille by the door and went out coming back in an hour later. It was now 2:00 am. It was time!

Chenille

Groggily awaken Chenille smiled when she noticed she was lying on something soft and she was no longer hanging from the fucking ceiling. By then the blizzard Sorrow gave her to paralyze her had worn off. She felt that her eyes were stuck together she pulled the tape off of them.

"Oh My fucking God! She screamed as she aimlessly pushed on the wood she was surrounded in, she heard a noise outside of the box, it was something falling on top, it started falling through the cracks. This bitch was burying her alive.

"Can anybody hear me? Help meeeee! Please help me."

Just then she heard a second voice a woman. Oh my god, this was her help. She screamed until she was hoarse.

Sorrow

Sorrow shoveling the dirt on top of Chenille, shovel by shovel, she managed to collect her feelings. She laughed at her screaming. No one could hear her not unless they were standing right next to her. Knowing this will be the end of her mother did not bring her joy as she would have thought. It was a mere task that needed to be done. Just like everyone else that she had killed.

It was a way to solve her longest going problem, an adversary she was born with and could not seem to get rid of. If she had the time she would have cut her up into 100 pieces and made sure she had 100 black coffins prepared for her. But, she was anxious to get back to her happiness, her family.

She could give two fucks about what she did to her, she had let that go when she thought she had buried her. But, of course, if you wanted something done right you had to do it your damn self.

So, here she was burying Chenille King the right way.

For the final time.

The thought of her being around her son, talking to him, corrupting him is what sent Sorrow over the edge. Nobody, wouldn't understand why she had to do this and why she had to do this herself. It took her 3 days to get this anger out of her, this revenge out on who took her children. Who would have thought it would be this evil bitch?

Buried alive!

What a fucking way to live and then die?

She was lost in her head.

"Ou pa janm bay tan lènmi ou pou tounen vin jwenn Bondye." She said walking up behind Sorrow with her gun aiming at the coffin.

Sorrow stopped shoveling and taped on the coffin, "My Grandme' is here to say hello, mother. Women in my family have a true gift of escaping death. Wouldn't you say so Mommie Dearest?" she laughed.

"Grandme', no disrespect but my enemy does not believe in God. How could a fucked up mother like her believe in a higher power? So, she wants to repent, she does not know how to repent. Do you mom? Do you know how to repent?"

Sorrow could still hear her screams and smiled.

"Bitch, now that we have evidence. Know I was always smarter than you bitch, even when I came out of your dirty ass pussy. The first thing I did was show your husband what a ho you were and a nasty ho at that fucking an engaged man without protection. With your nasty ass. You thought that what you saw was me killing someone I loved, the anarchy of my family. My kids only knew her as my Grandme', I show them pictures of my father's wife telling them she was my mom and their Grandma. And I will have no problems erasing you from their memories. I will just tell them you are now playing along came of hide and seek."

Chenille

"Fuck you! You Black Bitch, Fuck you! And your fucking Grandme'. Those kids loved me, they loved me." She screamed as she reached around to see if there was an opening, she needed to get out of there before the dirt completely sealed her inside the ground. She searched around and her hand hit something, it was a lighter. Oh, thank you, God, she mumbled to herself, she kept trying to flick it and when she did, her sleeve caught on fire. The fire rushed itself all over her clothes sucking up the gasoline her clothes were drenched in; she did not notice the smell at first.

You can hear her screams complete in disbelieve and anguish. She felt her flesh burning, she smelled her flesh burning, what a putrid aroma. She was burning alive.

Sorrow

Sorrow laughed as she heard her screams, she had found her gift. A Lighter! She had killed herself. Evelyn stood by her Black Beauty she did not pass judgment, but damn burying your mother alive and then giving her the tools to set herself on fire was, was genius to her. Evil. Evelyn had brought everyone in the Limo, she texted them to get out and come to the back.

Malakai, Nigel, Genesis all walked up from behind, holding guns with silencers on them. Nigel held two one for his wife and they all let bullets reign on top of the burning coffin even Evelyn joined in, for she too needed to avenge Chenille King's evil effect on her life.

By now, the whole coffin was burning, there wasn't any more screams or insults coming from the coffin. Nigel came and grabbed her hand, she looked up at him. She was looking for her big brother's approval because this was his mother also. He leaned over and kissed her on the forehead, "Hail Queen Black Panther he whispered to her. Their children were safe now, she was safe, and Nigel was safe because ding dong the evil bitch was dead.

Coda

The sunrise had graced the surface of not so quiet suburbs in Crown Point, Indiana, a SWAT team, Lake County Police and a slew of FBI men, and a Gary Police Homicide Detective surrounded the home of disgruntled Ex-Drug Force Detective. Everyone was awoken to the email with his video confession on it.

The SWAT team forced its way in to find Ex-Detective of the Gary Police Department Thomas Branson, beaten brutally to death. Black Lives Matter was written on the walls in blood. He had Scotch bottles at his feet and was sitting in his boxers, which would prove that the confession was real and not altered, the very person who had recorded him could be his killer but they had no evidence.

One Law Enforcement agent smiled to himself, knowing who and why but will never tell a soul. Matter of fact, he should commend him for doing his people and this world a service of justice. He had his gloves on, as he collected evidence he spotted a shoe print by Branson body he accidentally wasted fingerprint powder on top of it covering it up then he steps in it, no one was paying attention, he then bent down to Thomas's head, "That nigga beat your ass good. How does it feel to be killed by a black, mother fucker? I'm about to go celebrate." He laughed took off his gloves threw it on top of Branson's head and just walked away from the scene.

Nigel and Truth

Nigel and Semaj walked through the hospital room door, instantly Semaj ran to her mother, "Mommy! Mommy!, I miss you! She said trying to climb in the bed with her.

Truth eyes fluttered open with tears, "Oh my God, Baby Girl, I missed you too! She tried reaching out to her but the pain hit her, but she reached out and picked her up anyways, her pain was secondary to holding her little girl in her arms.

Nigel saw the struggle he ran over there to life Semaj into her mom's arms, he sat down and just watch them together. Semaj was telling her everything that happened with a smile on her face. Truth was comforted by the delight in her daughter's voice that meant no harm came to her. Truth had already been told who had the children. She found solace in knowing that Chenille didn't do anything to hurt her grandchildren.

Genesis, Nigel Jr., Sorrow, Malakai, and Hunter came in minutes later. Jr. came over to his Step-mom and said,"I'm glad you are okay, I couldn't lose two mommies."

Nigel patted Truth's hand to let her know that Jr. would be okay. She smiled, "Naw, son we couldn't let you lose two mommies. I'm sorry about your mom, I really am," she said sincerely.

"It's okay daddy, said that heaven is a way nicer place anyway."

"Hunter, come over here and give your Te-Te Truth some kisses."

"Aww, Te-Te Truth, I'm a big boy now, I can't be given out kisses in front of everybody." Hunter went over there anyways to get his kisses. They all laughed at his I'm a big boy antics.

Malakai and Sorrow were holding hands she winked at Truth because the kids and Nigel were surrounding her bed. Truth winked at her best friend back and mouthed, "Thank You So Much!"

Truth squeezed her daughter even tighter, Malakai wrapped his arms around Sorrow and whispered in her ear. "After we leave here we need to start back going to church but it was clearly God he got us through all of this."

Sorrow shook her head in agreement, "Do you want a girl or a boy?" She said pulling his hand on top of her stomach.

Tears filled his eyes and hers they were truly happy and God had blessed them to come out victories once again.

Genesis looked around and smiled, she felt the warmth and love of her family. Her phone had rung breaking the moment, she answered Sabrina's mother's number.

"Hello, Genesis this is Ms. Green, I was calling because Sabrina has been missing for a whole week now, the police suspect foul play. But anyhow she had left strict instructions on Cameron being with you. And I would like to abide by my daughter's wishes. So, whenever you are ready you can pick your son up."

"I'll be right there, Genesis said with tears in her eyes. She hung up.

Everybody looked at G as she knelt down and cried, "What's going on?" Sorrow asked. They had never seen her this way.

"Shit, she gave me custody of Cameron."

"At least that bitch had a little sense, Sorrow said without thinking. "I'm sorry G. Now the old Sorrow would have given one care that she disrespected her enemies but the new Sorrow toned her despise for people down. When she knew it would hurt the ones she loved.

"I can't get mad at facts. Let me go pick my son up. She said doing the cabbage patch out the room. They laughed their Congratulations to her as she danced out the door.

Genesis was stopped when she walked out, by this fine ass Puerto Rican nurse.
"Genesis, Right?"

"Hi, I'm Valentina. I was the head nurse taking care of you. Damn you look just as pretty as you- Well, it's nice to see you doing well."

"Thank you, for taking care of me! Genesis blushed.

"You welcome, well I just wanted to know can I give you my number."

Genesis looked at her, she was thick like she like them and she was fine like she loved them, "Hell, yeah!" she gave Valentina her phone to put her number in. When she gave it back she called her phone in return.

"Now, we both have access to each other anytime we want too." Genesis smiled and walked away.

Sorrow's Granparans (Grandparents) despite their hatred for American soil decided to stay in America to be closer to Sorrow and her family. They moved into the Miller Beach House. But they still had their Drug Empire in Haiti. Sorrow's Grandfather was safer in the USA anyway.

Sorrow had the house on 453 Jackson Street rebuild and expanded back over Chenille's grave and she turned it into a home for abused children. She smiled at the irony of it all.

The End